AN ISLAND BETWEEN TWO SHORES

This is a work of fiction. Names, characters, places, and incidents are the products of the author's imagination or are used fictitiously. Any resemblance to actual events, locales, or persons, living or dead, is entirely coincidental.

AN ISLAND BETWEEN TWO SHORES
by Graham Wilson
Copyright ©Graham Wilson
Edited by, Ann Chandonnet, Rebecca Grossman and Amelia
    Gilliland.
Cover Photograph by Ivan Bliznetsov.
Printed in the United States of America.

Library and Archives Canada Cataloguing in Publication
Wilson, Graham, 1962-
    An island between two shores / Graham Wilson.
ISBN 9781-927691-00-7

    I. Title.
PS8645.I46673I75 2010   C813'.6   C2010-
907336-3

FRIDAY 501

Box 31599, Whitehorse, Yukon, Canada, Y1A 6L2
www.friday501.com, info@friday501.com

ACKNOWLEDGEMENTS

I am indebted to the support of my family and friends. I would like to thank my daughters Emily, Jessica and Coco for their constant inspiration. I would also like to thank Sarah Sage, Deb and Bruce Bergman, Lloyd Ziff, Stephen Kelemen, Carson Schiffkorn, Tony Ciprani, Shanna Williams, Carol Geddes, Rod Leighton, Annie Avery, Mary Ann Lewis, Ross Wilson, Ewa Dembek, Brenda Lee Katerenchuck, Heather Stevely, Mark Abley, Susan Fournier, Sarah Sones, Rob Bergman, Robin and Sandy Burgess, Mary Beattie, David Jordan and Keith Webb.

G.W.

To my father

We have to continually be jumping off cliffs and developing our wings on the way down.
—KURT VONNEGUT

CONTENTS

Liana hid behind an ancient blind of grey green shale that was dusted with snow. Henry told her his people had built the blind since caribou had lived in the North. The simple ring of piled rocks had been strategically placed to provide an unobstructed view of the valley while hiding the hunter. It was ingenious, she thought; a simple, effective construction that had been passed down through the ages. She peeled off her leather glove and touched a thin stick that had been laid into the mossy wall. The stick was grey, coarse, and punky. Liana thought about Henry and his ancestors, who had built this blind and hunted in this valley using throwing sticks and spears. They probably even looked like Henry, she thought. Liana smiled, imagining Henry hunting with a spear in clothes made of caribou hides.

Liana thought about her old life in Paris. She remembered the sounds of the horses and carriages on the cobbled streets and the smells of the boulangerie and patisserie. She repeated the promise she made to herself so long ago to return to France when it was safe.

In the distance, snowy mountains shimmered in the mid-morning sun. She was startled by their enormity. The scale of the landscape was always unsettling to her. It was too vast, too expansive. This meadow was somewhere close to the border between Alaska and the Yukon, but she never cared to figure on which side it laid.

It was October, and a few inches of snow covered everything. She could see for many miles in every direction; there were only scattered stands of small pine and spruce. Mostly the meadow was low growing grasses and mosses, rhododendron, and dwarf birch covered by colourless snow.

Flexing her gloved fingers to restore their circulation, Liana crouched behind a boulder and waited for a clear shot of one of the cows. She had been waiting behind this cold chunk of granite for hours. The herd of sixteen caribou were slowly grazing their way up the meadow's gentle incline toward her hiding place. She wiggled her toes to keep the blood flowing and reassured herself that the herd would soon be within range of her rifle. She could hear the click and pop of their ankles. As hunters had done in this spot forever, she patiently bided her time.

She remembered Henry teaching her to hold and shoot the rifle. Liana was surprised by how poor his eyesight had been and what a good shot she was. But he would tease her that it didn't matter if a person was a crack shot if he wouldn't even kill a squirrel. Liana knew he was right and she would be able to fill their cache when the time came. They needed enough meat to last the winter, and going back to town was still out of the question.

Liana felt the anemic warmth of the sun through her heavy wool parka. The sky was pale grey but the morning's chill was gone. Liana was comfortable crouching and content to examine the distant mountains and the slow approach of the caribou. Even on this overcast day, her dark eyes squinted in the glare of the snow. Liana was only a little more than five feet tall, but her sinewy build was well suited to life in the bush. Her high cheekbones and slender nose gave some people the impression she was Scandinavian. But she was from Paris, her ancestors from Normandy.

The caribou used their front hooves to scrape through the light snow cover and expose shrubs, grasses, and lichen. Caribou moss was their favorite food, but this late in the season they ate almost anything. Soon the caribou were so close that Liana could hear them crunching and grinding their teeth on the tough, dry vegetation they ripped from the frozen ground. They were now so near that Liana feared looking over the blind, as the slightest movement might startle the herd. She was cautious of their hair trigger instinct for sensing danger. She intended to bide her time until they were almost within touching distance. In their surprise, a clear shot would be easier. Two or three caribou hung in the cache would feed them for the winter, since they already had salmon and a small moose dried. Still, Liana knew that caribou meat would be a welcome change, especially in the middle of winter when there wasn't much else to do than cook, drink tea, and talk.

Henry had taught her to shoot, but controlling her excitement was always a challenge when she was hunting. "Take a deep breath and pull the trigger slowly," he would tell her. "Don't squeeze the trigger. Make the first shot the kill shot." He was very serious when he spoke about hunting, as he hated to waste ammunition or see animals suffer. Whenever he set his marten traps, he would check them at least every day—sometimes more. In cold weather he would have to wear almost everything he had and strap on narrow snowshoes that were almost five feet long just to get to all the traps. Like most of the men of his generation, he made his snowshoes himself using birch saplings and babiche he rendered from a moose. The only tools he used were a hatchet, a knife, and a thin metal awl. Henry's snowshoes were as fine as any Liana had ever seen. She hoped that one day he would make her a pair so she could accompany him when the snows got deep. But for some reason he had never offered to make her a pair, and she wasn't so bold to ask.

Henry didn't like knowing that an animal could be in one of his traps, suffering for a long time. He told Liana that he sometimes found a bloody lynx or marten foot in his traps, indicating the animal had chewed its own foot to set itself free. This was a reality that he couldn't avoid. Nevertheless, he frequently checked his traps and carried a small club in case they were still alive.

In the dark, when Liana had left the cabin, she told Henry she would fire two shots if she was successful in shooting a caribou. This was their usual message. The echo from the blasts would tell Henry that she was butchering and need-ed help dragging the meat back to the cabin. Henry would pull a small sled to the plain, and together they would spend the day hauling a hundred pounds of the dark purple meat home. Liana felt it was a ritual of great intimacy. Her hunting was an act of commitment and sharing that allowed her and Henry to live their lives independently, away from the dan-gers of town. "I can do this," thought Liana. "I can get my first caribou." She had been on many hunts but had never killed anything herself.

Liana raised her head slowly from behind the stone blind until she could see that most of the herd had moved with-in fifty feet of her hiding place. One large cow was within twenty-five feet. The animal was oblivious to her presence as its long muzzle tugged on a dwarf birch. Just as Liana gen-tly slid the safety off her rifle, a distant gunshot rang in the morning still. Instinctively the caribou stopped feeding and raised their heads. The wary animals splayed their legs and looked at one another, tense with fear. "What's Henry doing?" thought Liana. The caribou exploded in flight and galloped across the meadow, sounding that distinctive click of their tendons as they moved toward a high ridge on the other side of the glade. Like a school of fish, the herd fled the meadow in dizzying unison. A second shot reverberated through the valley.

"Henry!" she shouted.

It occurred to her for the first time that Henry might be in trouble. He would never use his rifle when Liana was hunting caribou nearby. Something was wrong. Her mind raced with disturbing possibilities.

Liana slung her rifle over her shoulder by its braided leather strap and scrambled to gather her canteen, pack, and extra gloves. She took one last look at the caribou as they bounded toward the distant ridge on the far side of the plain. So little time had passed that their breath still hung in the meadow near her boulder blind.

The trail to the cabin was a winding path a couple of miles long. Liana ran along the flats of the meadow easily. Her path from the morning wound between low bushes and rocks. She glided across the plain in a quick sprint that hardly left her breathless. After several minutes of running on the flat trail she reached a treed gully that dropped steeply into the valley and the rocky bench where the cabin stood. A bulk of the gully sloped gently downward, but in a couple of places Liana had to face the trail and lower herself while hanging onto roots and branches so she didn't fall. The snow didn't allow much traction for her hobnailed leather boots, but Liana was running this path faster than she ever had before. It was a path she knew well, but because it was steep and snowy, her progress was much slower than it would have been weeks ago before the storms.

About a mile away she could see the yard and the roof of the cabin. She ran across the narrow ridge, following her tracks and the occasional blaze on the trees. Within five minutes she was directly above the cabin. She could see two men standing outside. Instinctively, she hid behind the bushes and slowed her breathing to prevent the sound of her gasps from carrying to the strangers.

The men were standing over something, but Liana couldn't tell what it was. She craned her neck, searching for Henry in the yard. "Perhaps he's down at the creek?" she hoped. Suddenly Liana recognized Henry's grey flannel shirt; it was his favorite. It was draped over the shape heaped in the snow at the men's feet. Henry was lying motionless on his stomach. The men were talking; one smoked a pipe.

Liana crawled closer, concealing herself behind a boulder. She slipped her rifle off her shoulder. Her stomach convulsed at the thought that Henry had been murdered. She wretched quietly into the snow. Tears ran down her cheeks and her mind raced. Liana watched one man reached under Henry's armpits and drag his limp body into the cabin. A bright red stain in the fresh snow marked where he had fallen. Liana took this opportunity to move closer to the cabin without the man with the pipe seeing her. Staying crouched, she carefully crept between the small boulders on the ridge. She knew she would be exposed but had to get closer to Henry.

Liana managed to scurry to within a few hundred yards of the homestead. Smoke started to billow out of the cabin's front door. In an instant she saw small flames race across the floor and the three men exited hastily. A lick of flames enveloped the lace curtains she had sewn by hand. The blaze filled the windows. Liana watched in disbelief as the cabin blazed with an inferno that growled as it consumed. The men stepped backwards, feeling the heat and talking amongst themselves over the roar of the flames.

The man with the pipe seemed to sense something and turned to scan the yard. Immediately he noticed Liana, half-concealed behind a small boulder on the ridge line above. Their eyes met. Liana quickly stood, raised her rifle, and sighted the man. As Henry had taught her, she pulled—rather than squeezed—the trigger, but at the last moment she shifted the barrel to the left and the bullet disappeared into the forest. The man recoiled and instinctively fell to the ground. Liana knew this man. He worked for Cody. She didn't know his name; she had only seen him standing on the porch of Cody's saloon. The other man, fearing for his own safety, took cover behind the log food cache. Liana knew she didn't have a clear shot. Making an instant decision about the safest course of action, she slung her rifle on her shoulder and retreated the way she had come, crouching low all the while.

The men stayed concealed for a few moments and then realized Liana was on the run. The man with the pipe hollered, "You better just give up. We won't hurt ya!" But Liana didn't even slow her pace as she scrambled up the gully. She knew they would kill her, too. Cody's men were ruthless; everyone knew that. The men began to take shots at Liana, but she didn't slow her scramble across the ridge. The popping thunder of rifle fire filled the sky, but Liana had already reached the base of the gully and temporary safety.

She started her climb up the gully. She peered around the wide trunk of a spruce tree and saw the men running toward the start of the ridge. Soon they would cross the trail. Liana turned into the gully and scurried over roots and small boulders. It was a long, difficult ascent and the slipperiness of the new snow only made it more challenging. However, Liana was made for northern terrain and with little effort she covered the ground, leaping from rock to rock. Never looking back, she followed the path through the boulders and up the steep gully. The terrain gained a thousand vertical feet with relentless gradient. Her breathing was laboured and her mind was cluttered with images of Henry's death and the burning cabin. She could no longer hear or see the men but she knew they were behind her, following her unmistakable tracks through the snow.

Within fifteen minutes, Liana reached the end of the small ridge and began to climb the path back to the vast meadow where she had waited for the caribou. Her breath was heavy and her brow covered in sweat. She had regained control of her breath by swallowing massive gulps of air. Her footfall was quick, deliberate, and paced. The narrow trail wound its way up the steep hill and soon she would be on the treeless plain.

When Liana crested the gully she could see the men struggling to keep up. They were far below at the base of the steep ascent. Instead of running across the plain, she decided to find a place to snipe at the murderers. She ran across the rim above the gully to gain a good vantage point. Carefully she found a large spruce tree that allowed her a good view of the upper gully. She took another brass bullet from her breast pocket and reloaded her rifle. The men hurried between the boulders in the gully while Liana gradually caught her breath. Her heart raced and her mind felt light from the shock of having just lost everything that mattered to her. She was determined to survive—and have her revenge. Henry's death would be paid for.

She rested quietly until the men's deep voices could be heard. She couldn't make out what they were saying, though it sounded as if they were breathing hard. As they climbed over a particularly steep part of the trail by pulling themselves up using an exposed tree root, Liana once again raised her rifle. She couldn't look. She squeezed the trigger blindly. The thundering gunshot reverberated in the gully and the men scurried behind boulders. Instinctively, both of her pursuers cowered.

Hearing the men again in frantic conversation, Liana stepped back from the gully so as not to be seen and scanned the vast plain. She shouldered her gear and followed the trail through the meadow. She knew that as soon as the men reached the top of the gully she would be exposed and they would have a clear shot at her. Hopefully they would fear her shots and stay hidden long enough for her to get down the trail. There was nowhere to hide and her telltale tracks through the snow would lead them wherever she went.

Resolve imbued her with strength, and she ran across the frozen meadow on fresh legs. The day had advanced to mid afternoon and the pale sunlight left no shadows on the crisp snow. Liana knew that she would be vulnerable on the plain and ran an aggressive pace through the light snow. Her rifle bounced on her shoulder and her mouth felt gummy with saliva.

She was halfway across the enormous meadow when the two men crested the gully. They had slowed their progress in fear of an ambush from above. In the distance they could see Liana running across the open plain. She was almost a third of the way across the meadow and the two men had just reached the edge of the stretch. She was out of range of their rifles, but they knew they had her trapped. The river on the other side of the plain was impassable. If they could keep her in the open, they could track her to the river, where she would be trapped.

The plain was tabletop flat. During the summers, Larkspur, Jacob's ladder, and Monkshood were everywhere. Sometimes Henry and Liana would picnic there. They would spread a blanket and eat biscuits smothered with blueberry jam, made with berries she collected each August on the plain. They would kindle a small fire and brew a pot of black coffee. Then they would lie on their backs and watch the clouds cross above them, usually cresting the mountains to the east and tracking to the northwest. For sweet, lazy hours, Henry would tell her Indian stories that had been passed down by his people. These afternoons were the happiest times of Liana's life.

Liana stopped momentarily at the stone hunting blind and saw the footprints left by the caribou. She scampered on top of the boulder she had hid behind earlier in the day and could see the men following doggedly. Liana looked in the distance but couldn't see the caribou. She glanced at the alpine ridges that flanked the plain and considered climbing higher but knew the men could easily follow her tracks and close in on her. Then she remembered the canoe Henry had stashed on the pebble beach near the river for the winter. She could follow the blazes on the other side of the river and escape. With renewed vigor, Liana picked up her pace.

As she ran, Liana considered that if the men knew she was running for the canoe, they could position themselves on the bluff over the river and simply pick her off. She couldn't cross in daylight and night was still a few hours away. She would have to hide, but they could track her wherever she went. Beyond the tree line, she stood as exposed as the caribou.

Liana thought about all the hunting stories Henry had told her during the long winter nights. As she ran, her mind raced for a way to hide. "Henry!" she muttered in frustration. "What do I do now? Help me!" She knew she was exposed in the wide open plain and kept her pace strong, but she feared she was running into a trap.

As she sprinted over the frozen meadow she remembered Henry and the near-perfect life she was now being forced to abandon. Henry was dead. Everything was finished. Liana felt a pain in her chest but didn't allow herself to slow down; she knew that she had to get as much distance from the men as possible before reaching the other side of the plain.

Henry always cautioned Liana not to rush things. "Take your time. Be sure of everything." was his counsel. Liana remembered these astute words and was comforted by them. She pushed her hair from her forehead and thought about Cody. Not in her darkest dreams could she ever have imagined Cody would have Henry shot. "Cody grubstaked Papa on his claim," she thought. "It doesn't make any sense."

Liana paused momentarily to turn and look back. The men were walking fast and had already covered almost half a mile of the plain, seemingly without breaking into so much as a jog. They were moving single file along Liana's trail and would be closing in more quickly than she anticipated. She knew these men would kill her without hesitation. But Liana had more than a mile on them now and if she kept up her pace she might be able to extend the lead by more than two miles before reaching the river valley. Liana turned and started running again, slightly faster than before. Her feet were wet from the snow and her boots weighed enough that her calf muscles cried out in exhaustion.

When Liana finally reached the valley, the forest was a welcome relief. She could see the blaze marking the way to the canoe but she knew the men could as well. "It's a well-known crossing," she thought. "Besides, they're too close for me to paddle across the river without being shot." Liana felt trapped. The only way out was to go downhill to the river. She looked at the men one last time and could see one of them walking away from the other toward a bluff above the river. "They must know about the canoe," she whispered over her panting breath. "The snare is set."

Liana took a chunk of brown sugar from her pocket, popped it into her mouth, and started to run. She dropped into the valley with its tall spruce and pine trees. Every fifty feet was Henry's blaze, a tidy bright axe cut oozing bright sap. Liana jumped from rock to rock. To steady herself, she grabbed saplings and bushes as best she could and carefully followed the trail. Her descent was haphazard and she sensed the hopelessness of her task. The trail seemed too brief and soon she could hear the gentle hush of the river. A little farther down the trail, she got her first glimpse of steely grey water through the snow-covered branches. This sight gave her pause. Cody's men would close in soon.

As Liana climbed over a small ridge, an opening in the side of the hill caught her eye. "It must be a bear den," she thought. She had travelled this trail with Henry a month earlier while fishing for salmon and had not noticed the den. "That's something Henry wouldn't have missed. It must be fresh," Liana considered.

She walked down the trail about a hundred yards then stopped and followed her tracks, walking backwards in her steps. She carefully stepped backward into her footprints until she reached the entrance to the den. It appeared as though her tracks ended, a ruse she knew would fool the men only momentarily. Liana peered into the dim opening but could see nothing. She turned her head and listened for the breathing of a slumbering bear but did not hear anything. Looking up the trail and fearing the men were going to appear at anytime, she lifted her leg into the bear den and then carefully crawled into its narrow mouth.

Poised to flee, she paused momentarily and listened to make sure the den was empty. Still hearing nothing, Liana slid inside and scrambled her legs back from the entrance into the darkness. Lying on her side in the dim, earthy interior, she slowly cocked her rifle and waited for her enemy. She lay motionless for what seemed like an eternity. She wondered if the men had already discovered her game and were positioning themselves to easily kill her by shooting into the den. Then she heard it: a gentle sigh. With her left hand she carefully felt the ground behind her. There was a small rise to a higher platform. To her horror, she could smell its dense musk and feel the damp warmth of its massive presence. Now she could hear its deep, rhythmic breathing. Within a few feet of her was a grizzly bear, deep in the sleep of winter. Liana's head swam with the complexities of this new and dangerous situation. Momentarily she forgot about the men who hunted her.

She remembered Henry telling her that unlike black bears, grizzlies don't hibernate but merely sleep. Periodically they wake in the winter and occasionally attack people. Those that did were called Winter Bears and scared everybody with their bloodthirstiness. Henry never hunted bears, but he told Liana stories about how his people woke dening bears and when the beasts charged, ran them through with long spears anchored into the crook of a tree root. Liana hoped this one was in a very deep sleep. She stayed frozen still and held her breath, her heart pounding in her ears.

The entrance of the den seemed bright and Liana waited for the men to pass in front. It took several minutes before she heard a stick break and could see a man's dark jacket pass a few feet in front of the den. Dark, curly hair dangled from under a black leather hat. She watched him walk to the end of her trail where her tracks vanished. In confusion he turned to face back up the trail. The man shouted into the forest "Come out, come out, wherever you are" and then raised the muzzle of his rifle into the air and fired a single shot. A deafening ring and flash of light filled the den. Musky air enveloped Liana as the enormous bear pushed past her as if she didn't exist and escaped, half-dozing, from the den. Liana was thrown to the ridge outside the cave by the charging bear. Liana rolled forward several times down the steep hill and inadvertently dropped her rifle in the snow. She tumbled down the hill trying to get away from the rampaging bear as quickly as possible.

The confused bear raced at the man. Startled, he froze at the sight of the enormous bruin bearing down on him. Before he could get off a shot, the grizzly was on him. The man shrieked in horror as the bear knocked him onto his back and with a single swipe of its enormous paw swept the man's jaw from his face. Now wide awake, the bear roared as it ripped into the man's neck. Blood pulsing from his throat.

When Liana stopped rolling, she was thirty feet away from the den and only ten feet from the bear. The grizzly was studying her. Its broad face dripped with blood, and its tiny eyes looked as confused and shocked as Liana's. Shaking its head, it snarled and again tore into the man. Liana backed downhill toward the canoe. The bear, distracted by the warm body in its jaws, ignored Liana's escape. She tumbled the final distance down the slippery hill to the river.

At the bottom of the hill she could see the red canoe resting in the crux of an aspen tree. It would be dark soon. She could launch the canoe under the cover of night and escape the man on the bluff. In preparation, Liana flipped the canoe to conceal its red hull from above and slid it close to the river. She laid the paddle in the canoe and examined the distant shore. It was a large river and the current would wash her downstream. She thought about her options. She didn't know anything about the river and assumed it didn't have any rapids. Maybe she could race the man back to Dawson City by paddling down the river. She could easily beat a man on horseback by a day or so. "Cody won't know what hit him if I got to town first," she thought.

Liana trudged upstream along the snow-covered gravel beach, her feet wet, heavy, and cold. She kept close to a low-cut bank to stay out of sight of the high bluff. Aside from the spot where they fished for salmon, there wasn't anything on that side of the river that seemed familiar. She couldn't see very far but knew the man could draw a bead on her from anywhere. She imagined he waited for his opportunity somewhere out of sight. Liana scanned the far side of the river looking for a miracle but found nothing. Shivering with exhaustion and grief, Liana felt as helpless as a rabbit dangling in a snare.

She climbed onto the ice on a bend of the river and walked along the river partially concealed by the vegetation that bordered the beach. Since the ice wasn't covered in snow, Liana felt comforted that she wasn't leaving tracks.

A short distance upstream, she noticed a cavern created by the river undercutting the bank. The tree that had been felled by the erosion of the river was long gone and she knew she had found her sanctuary. Liana climbed into the tiny grotto and pulled her legs to her chest to hide in the shadows. She tried to catch her breath and sucked air through her clenched teeth. Liana wondered if the man would be able to follow her tracks over the ice. At that moment, the silence was shattered by a rifle blast and a shriek from the bear. Another blast roared through the valley before the forest went silent.

Liana considered running again but knew her motion would be noticeable and the man would be able to snipe her from the hillside above. A few moments later she saw the darkened silhouette of the man following her trail up the river. Her pursuer stepped onto the ice sheet bordering the river. Liana pulled her legs tightly against her chest and drew herself as far into the undercut as she could. She heard—but did not see—the jagged fracture rip through the ice under the man's weight; he slid helplessly into the water with a large splash. Peaking her head around, Liana watched as the man reached an arm out of the river in a desperate attempt to climb onto the ice sheet. His face spluttered to the surface and he tried to bounce off the bottom and onto the ice. The current resisted these efforts and the man was dragged downstream. His struggles for breath were muffled as he drifted away.

The forest was silent once again. Liana stared at the darkening forest in disbelief as daylight slowly faded.

nce night fell, Liana warily pushed Henry's canoe over the ice and into the river with barely a sound. Since the moon hadn't risen, the river was pitch black and Liana felt the current turn the canoe to face downstream as soon as she stepped on board. She wasn't sure if another man waited on the bluff, so she only took a couple of strokes to get into the current and away from the ice along the shore. She gently placed the paddle into the canoe and cowered on the floor of the boat. Liana held her breath and watched for any sign of motion as she let the river whisk her downstream past the bluff. She expected the flash of gunpowder at any moment. After she passed the bluff, she sighed in relief and sat up in the canoe. She picked up the paddle and took several hesitant strokes.

To be safe, Liana kept the canoe in the middle of the river and away from an easy shot from shore. When the moon rose she would be able to see the great forest on either side of the river and could position the canoe closer to the far shore. The twilight path of rushing water swept her through the maze of the shadowy forest. Her thoughts frequently returned to Henry and their burning home. Hatred for Cody seethed inside her. Her ears felt hot whenever she thought about him. It was a long night and only these thoughts occupied her mind.

She had a vague idea where she was and hoped the river wouldn't meander too much and would take her to town as quickly as possible. Eventually the moon set behind the mountains and the corduroy texture of the alpine ridges filled with the luster of morning. Her rhythmic paddling kept her warm and the daylight made Liana feel renewed. So far she had seen no sign of pursuit and knew she was far enough away from her pursuers that she wouldn't be ambushed now.

Liana climbed over a thwart to the middle of the canoe and sat on the floor. She lowered herself backward and laid on the bottom of the boat. The morning sky was pale and only a few wispy clouds floated overhead. Liana closed her eyes for a few minutes and basked in the muted warmth of the sun. Her deep exhaustion and hunger washed over her like a wave, but the gentle tug of the current kept her from resting.

Liana sat up after a few minutes and looked around to ensure she wasn't too close to shore. She was surprised by how far she had drifted with the current. The brusque, wintry breeze and the moist air over the river sandpapered her face and hands; she felt raw.

Liana always thought of Henry as an old man, but now she remembered him moving through the forest as spryly as a teen. His face was lined, but his crooked smile was ever accessible and warm. His blood in the snow and the acrid smoke from their burning cabin crowded her thoughts. Liana felt sorry for herself, if only for a moment.

Her hands were blue-white from gripping the paddle and from time to time she placed them under her armpits to try to warm them enough to grip the paddle again. Her hands tingled as they slowly thawed. Her stomach groaned and she felt weak in the stark, looming landscape. Drifting in the current made her feel depressed and she tried not to dwell on sad thoughts. She picked up her paddle and felt her stomach stretch as she dug into the stroke.

Liana looked at the shore and tried to figure out how quickly she was traveling. She knew she always walked a pace of at least three miles per hour, and it appeared she was easily traveling twice that speed. She felt impatient with canoeing and wanted to get to town as quickly as possible. Without provisions, a tent, or bedroll, she felt exposed. Henry was dead and it was her fault. He had been her father's friend and was trying to help her. For several hours, Liana pushed herself to dig her paddle into the coppery river again and again. Her arms and back were exhausted and tight. Her determination gave her a break from thinking about Henry, but her energy was starting to wane.

"At higher water this river must really move," she thought as she finally took another break and drifted in the current. The canoe slowly turned and Liana faced upstream. The distant mountains near where the cabin once stood slowly faded into the distance. She drifted past trees and bluffs that all seemed to look the same, and she was losing the mountainous reference she had come to know so well. Liana closed her eyes briefly and tucked her chin to her chest. She felt the gentle wobble of the canoe in the current. Stopping for a nap on shore wasn't an option, as she needed to get to town before the man—where is he? she wondered. The current dragged her through the forest and mountains while her back throbbed with fatigue.

After several minutes, Liana opened her eyes and studied the dappled ripples of the river. Its motion made her feel dizzy, and she closed her eyes and thought about Henry. She felt comforted by the kindness he had shown her, despite the burden of pain he carried. He had told her once that his wife and two daughters had died, like many others, during an *influenza* outbreak. He was away from the village, cutting wood for a paddlewheeler company, and only learned of their passing a few weeks after their burial. What surprised Liana was the fact that Henry only told her this story once and didn't seem to dwell on his sadness. He smiled a toothy grin when he spoke of them and Liana knew not to ask questions. She understood what it meant to lose a family.

Henry's canoe was red cedar and its rich grain sparkled under a shiny coat of shellac. In places the coating had blistered, but most of it was in good shape. Its bright ash gunwales gleamed in the afternoon light and the boat felt sturdy but agile. A thin layer of canvas, waterproofed with vibrant red paint, protected the hull. This sort of craft was used everywhere in the North. At sixteen feet, the boat was designed to carry a lone trapper and his bale of furs to distant trading posts. This canoe could take rapids and large lakes equally well. It could be portaged relatively easily when flipped and placed over one's shoulders. At night it could be propped against a tree or rock to make a shelter.

Liana rested her paddle across the gunwale and tucked her hands into her armpits. She stretched her legs straight in front of her. She felt alone. Tears welled in her eyes and a deep moan resonated from her belly. For several minutes, she sobbed resignedly. "Alone again," she thought.

When Liana's hands had warmed, she picked up the maple paddle and took several short deliberate strokes to turn the canoe downstream and toward the town. The paddle belonged to Henry and was too long for her. It felt awkward in her small hands. Liana grew tired of watching the forest and turned her attention to the river bottom. She watched the pink, grey, and brown rocks covering the bottom. As the rocks sped by they made Liana feel slightly faint, and this feeling was strangely comforting to her. Liana was moving more quickly through the great forest and she watched the trees speed by. It would only be a matter of time before she saw another cabin or reached town.

The forest that lined the river was immense. Gnarled trees covered the mountains nearly to their tops. The treeless crests of the mountains were now dense with snow. This late in the season, the snow already covered the mountain to its base at the river. It would not be long before ice spread across the river and the current stopped.

Liana paddled with her collar pulled high and her hat pulled low on her brow. Her feet were numb and wet and her entire being ached with fatigue. Liana's stomach grumbled with profound emptiness and she licked her dry, cracked lips. She had only one chunk of sugar remaining, and she carefully took it out of her pocket and placed the amber ball on her tongue. The sugar quickly dissolved and Liana felt the sweetness fill her mouth. It wasn't enough but it was a welcome treat, and for a moment she felt everything was going to be fine.

Liana remembered a neighbour of theirs in Dawson whom her father thought was very strange. This man lived in a small log home near the downtown. In his home he kept a wide variety of tropical plants. There were more plants than you could imagine, their drippy branches and leaves draping over everything, threatening to break out the windows to escape. The man had built an elaborate wood heating system whereby a wood furnace would heat water that would circulate throughout his home. He sent away for seeds and cuttings from all over the world. When they arrived he would carefully add compost to a clay pot of soil and try to create a home for the transplant. His prize was an orange tree from seeds from Florida. The strange thing was the way the plants grew despite the months of darkness. With effort, the man kept the house warm by feeding the furnace with cord upon cord of wood. Seemingly no amount of effort could replace the nourishing rays of sunlight, yet his plants seemed to do all right and some even thrived in these rarified conditions. He always remarked that the jungle floor is dark as well, and Liana wondered if that was true or not as she had never seen a jungle. Her father often said that the man should just move somewhere in the south where his life would be easier and better. "If you want tropical plants, move to the tropics," he said with exasperation. Liana had never been inside the house but had glimpsed the veritable rainforest through the frosted windows. She craved life inside this warm, moist house over-grown with foliage and heating pipes.

Autumn days are brief in the North. As the sun dropped behind the mountains, Liana braced herself for another night of cold and moonlight. The pitch black of a new moon was disorienting with its absoluteness. She had paddled many times with Henry under the full moon when they went moose hunting in the fall. They paddled in the dark to get to Henry's favourite hunting swamp. Liana always liked paddling in the dark with Henry; they would talk softly and drink strong coffee before setting out. Those were very different nights from this, Liana thought.

Liana pulled hard with each stroke to get to town as quickly as possible. She thought about eating but decided it was best to keep moving rather than stop to forage. She didn't try to fish, even though she had a hook and line in her bag, and she didn't go to shore to find any berries, rose hips, or roots. She had left her rifle at the bear den and seeing any wildlife wouldn't help her now. Instead, she mustered her strength to rhythmically paddle as far as possible each hour. Liana wanted to leave the forest and the North and the pain. She waited patiently all night for the brightness of morning.

Liana expertly used the J-stroke to keep the canoe tracking in a straight line. As she pulled the paddle toward herself she gave it a light flick to correct the canoe's tendency to turn to the outside. She pulled in tight, powerful strokes and the hardwood paddle flexed expertly with each pass in the river. This slight flex absorbed much of the shock of the stroke, but Liana still felt exhausted. Imperceptibly, the low ridges next to the river were becoming more congested. At the same time the river was gaining speed. Liana was unaware of these subtle changes as she paddled deep in her grim thoughts. Gradually the dark was replaced by the pale of an overcast morning.

As Liana paddled she sang "Au Clair de la Lune" in a breathless little voice. It was a song her mother had taught her. The words of the song were lost in the repetitions of her paddle strokes and the meaning of the words a stark reminder of everything she had lost. It comforted her to remember her parents and the three of them enjoying pain au chocolate and hot cocoa on the balcony of their Paris apartment.

In the light of the moon, Pierrot, my friend
Loan me your pen to write something down
My candle's dead, I've got no flame to light it
Open your door, for the love of God!

In the light of the moon, Pierrot replied
I don't have a pen, I'm in bed
Go to the neighbor's, I think she's there
Because someone just lit a match in the kitchen

In the light of the moon, likable Harlequin
Knocked on the brunette's door, and she responded immediately
Who's knocking like that? And he replied
Open your door, for the God of Love!

In the light of the moon, you can barely see anything
Someone looked for a pen, someone looked for a flame
In all of that looking, I don't know what was found
But I do know that those two shut the door behind them.

The ridges and snow-covered mountains formed a jagged boundary to the pale, cloudless sky. The looming forest bordering the river was covered in a dusting of snow. The water level of the river was low, and snow-covered gravel bars and beaches appeared around each bend. The leafless willow trees strained under the weight of the snow. The sun no longer gave much warmth and Liana pulled her collar up farther to protect her cheeks from the crisp, dry air. The fragile autumn landscape had lost most of its energy and everything seemed to slow. Alone and full of grief, Liana couldn't leave fast enough.

Liana continued to paddle, unaware that the river was changing. A low bank next to the right hand shore gradually became a ten-foot cliff. Spring floods and seasons of ice had polished its pink face smooth. The shift was too faint for Liana to notice, especially as she punctuated her rhythmic paddling with nearly obsessive recitations of "Au Clair de la Lune." Inattentiveness can exact a bitter price.

About half a mile farther downstream, a low bank on the left side of the river also rose into a low pink overhang. This change was imperceptible and gradual; Liana paid it no notice. However, the river—and Liana—were now trapped between these two rocky crags. These small cliffs would have continued as far as Liana could see if she had been paying attention. The river coursed through the canyon for several violent miles. There was no escape.

Liana paddled downstream unaware of her fate. The river gradually quickened with the occasional small crashing wave. The rocky cliff's fractured face slowly gained height until it towered twenty-five feet above the river. It was at this point that it dawned on Liana that she might be in a new kind of trap. Liana snapped out of her dreamy recollections and felt the gravity of her plight.

Shaking herself, she studied the cliffs on either side of her and accepted that she was likely walled in. Her heart raced as she searched for a spot to land the canoe, but the river did not give any respite and coursed without bend as it approached a high, black bluff. The imposing monolith towered high above the river. She then remembered that Henry had once spoken of a fearsome canyon he called "The Fox" because "it sneaks up on you." But that was all she could remember. Liana frantically tried to recollect what else Henry had said as she searched for a break in the canyon walls.

The river took a dogleg and went abruptly left. As the water piled onto the right bank, a maelstrom of waves and foam threatened. Frantically Liana sought an eddy to land the canoe but there wasn't any respite in the sheer walls and menacing rapids. Instinctively, she moved off the seat of the canoe and splayed her knees apart on the hull to better balance her weight. She continued to paddle quickly as she searched the riverbanks for a landing to escape the turbulence a half-mile away. She pointed the canoe to the left shore. In short, deliberate strokes she worked the canoe toward the cliff face. When she was about ten feet from the wall, she scoured hopelessly for any break in the constancy of the canyon. Its walls towered high above the river and the water churned between the cliffs was cast in a menacing shadow. Liana looked downstream and could smell the freshness of the rapids. She gritted her teeth in dismay.

As Liana neared the black cliff, the deep hush of the rapids filled her. A grey groan that would be a roar sounded farther downstream. The sound of the rapids had been muffled behind the cliffs until she reached this point. In horror she heard the unmistakable call of churning waters. In the distance she could see the telltale spit of a hole. She knew that holes could be treacherous. The water drops over a ledge and travels deep along the bottom of the river only to surface and go back upstream toward the ledge and then folds in on itself. Liana knew a hole could recirculate her in its froth and there wouldn't be an escape. The farther the canoe bobbed into the canyon, the louder the rapids became. Still, the river itself was eerily placid as it approached the exploding rapids. Liana could see that the calm would break in the next half mile, when the river entered its first big bend since the monolith. She knew it was going to explode with ferocity and her mind raced with panic.

In desperation she once again headed for shore. She aimed the bow of the canoe toward the left-hand bend since she knew that currents always flow more slowly on the inside of a corner. Liana turned the canoe broadside to the current and started to pull herself to shore using short, quick strokes. But the canyon walls continued without a break and there was no escape. Liana had unwittingly committed herself to challenging the sly "Fox." Liana pulled her hat snuggly over her ears, buttoned her heavy woolen jacket, and said a soft prayer. "Hail Mary, full of grace…"

Standing waves began to appear randomly on both sides of the river. The canyon walls felt even more imposing. At first Liana could see the large, glassy faces of the waves from a distance and could maneuver to avoid them. But as she paddled farther into the canyon, powerful eddies and waves were more frequent and less avoidable.

She saw the first hole shortly after she rounded the corner almost directly underneath the canyon wall. It was about twenty feet wide and it seemed a third of the river sank abruptly into it. Liana furiously paddled to miss its exploding mass, and as she passed this danger she gaped into its deep, surging white maw from about fifteen feet away. The hole was about six feet deep with a long glissade dropping into its trough of ferocious turbulence. Liana knew that a hole like this would finish her off in an instant. It was a horrible sight and Liana feared other watery graves lurking ahead.

The occasional wave at the entrance to the canyon was now replaced by long sets of wave trains. Wave behind wave behind wave came with dizzying, unavoidable regularity. She paddled hard but tried to slow her progress and prevent swamping the canoe by paddling backwards. At the apex of each wave, Liana looked downstream to consider which waves she could avoid and which waves were unavoidable. She desperately scanned the horizon to view any breaks in the canyon wall. There were none. She dropped low into another wave and another and another. The canoe dipped into each trough and slowly climbed the crest, only to drop into another waiting trough on the other side.

The canyon walls towered above her with dizzying steepness. The top of the canyon was lined with a dense wall of forest. The river ricocheted from wall to wall against an unbroken veil of vertical rock. Liana no longer searched for an escape and instead resigned herself to her uncertain fate. Ahead were unknown miles of explosive rapids.

After several S-bends, Liana was breathing hard and growing insurmountably weary. Her chest throbbed wildly and her ears rang from the monotonous groan of the rapids. Terror filled her as she charged, uncontrolled, through the din. The canoe bobbed in the rapids like an eggshell. With each wave, the hull swallowed more and more water and was beginning to labor under the extra weight. Water sloshed around Liana's soaked feet and calves and exaggerated the turbulence of the river by pitching and rolling in the waves.

Liana's attention was suddenly rapt by what appeared to be a piece of wood painted red high up on the cliff face. It was almost fifty feet higher than the river, embedded in a line that indicated an old flood during which the river had run that high.

She pounded another breaking wave and slid down its backside. She refocused her attention on the river and with each stroke came closer to surviving the canyon. The waves cresting into steep, haystack-sized white shapes. It was a jumble of waves building and crashing flat in a disorganized mess of foam.

Liana paddled in desperation in quick stabs and braces. She knew that flipping a canoe in this canyon meant almost certain death. If she didn't drown outright, she would freeze in minutes. She dug her paddle into the river and did her best to keep the canoe pointing downstream. When the waves were really big, she slowed the canoe to limit the amount of water that splashed over the gunwales, but every seep of water saw her chances of survival dwindle. "When will the canyon end?" she pleaded to the waves. The roar of the rapids filled her heart, while her leaden arms frantically flailed her paddle through the turbulence.

After many bends and countless chaotic waves Liana saw what appeared to be the end of the canyon. The right canyon wall ended as abruptly as it had begun, the shear face dropping to the river and allowing the forest to creep to the river's edge. Liana's heart opened; she had made it; she had survived the canyon. She felt joyous as she crashed and bobbed in the last of the rapids. All she needed to do was survive the next quarter-mile of river and she would be free. Liana crested wave after wave with a refreshed sense of optimism.

On the last bend she noticed that the soft moan of the river had changed. Liana heard a roar louder than anything she had experienced so far, but she couldn't see where it came from until she peered downstream from the crest of a large, rolling wave. To her horror, an enormous hole lay directly ahead. Most of the river spilled into it and she was headed straight for its maw. Liana changed the direction of the canoe, pointing it to the right-hand shore. As she did this, she climbed a long, smooth wave. When she reached its apex, the canoe stalled for an instant and the shuddering craft unintentionally turned broadside on the crest. Liana tried to correct this mistake with a powerful stroke, but it was too late. Liana and the canoe slid down the wave's backside into a dark standing wave with a huge white crest. Liana dropped her paddle and gripped the canoe's gunwales in desperation. The wave spilled its enormity into the canoe and in an instant the craft was swamped with icy water.

With a gasp at its coldness, Liana felt the water flood to her waist and then the canoe sank a few feet into the current. Unable to help herself, Liana washed out of the canoe and it slowly turned on its side. The arctic river stole Liana's breath and she struggled for air. She watched her canvas duffel pack float away and disappear. As Liana gasped and spluttered for breath, she bobbed helplessly over the waves. Suddenly, the gunwale of the canoe rose near her right hand. She grabbed it and tried to climb on top of the overturned hull, but the canoe sank beneath her and Liana let go.

Liana knew her chances of surviving the rapid were practically nil. She cursed having failed so close to the end of the ordeal. The cold was already sinking into her core and she could feel her last reserves of energy fading. In a few moments she would be in the hole. Strangely, she felt at peace with her situation.

About thirty feet upstream of the hole Liana crested a large wave and could see the enormity of it for the first time. The hole surged almost mechanically and Liana took one last gasp as she dropped over the lip and slid into the exploding maw. She closed her eyes as she plunged weightlessly into the void and was swallowed by its icy turbulence. Liana tumbled violently in the foam below the surface of the river. The frothing face of the collapsing wave forced her to spin wildly several times. At first the water was white and turbulent and then everything became dark and still. The sound of the rapids finally quieted, and she was washed to the surface of the river. Amazed by her luck and that she was still alive, Liana gasped for breath as her face broke the calm surface of the river. Liana had been spit out of the hole and into its wash. She could see daylight and hear the rapids fade slowly into the distance.

Liana looked upstream and could see the canoe was still in the hole. It spun helplessly end over end. Then the canoe stood almost straight up in the air momentarily before it broke into two pieces with a sudden thrust.

She gasped for air and kicked her feet. The cold water made all her motions feel exaggerated and pointless. She was being pushed downstream while watching the carnage in the canyon when her feet hit something. It was a rock. At the same time, her knee painfully glanced another rock. She turned her head and saw that she had washed onto a small island. She struggled onto her knees and slowly crawled up the snow-covered gravel. She lay on her side, heaving water and convulsing.

Liana shivered uncontrollably, her lips blue, and slowly stood to face the river. Trying to gather her wits, she staggered away from the bank to an enormous log and collapsed beside it. She sat still for several minutes in disbelief.

Liana reached for the knife she wore on her waist. With relief she felt the familiar rosewood handle of her father's blade; it gave her a sense of security. She took it from its sheath and held it in the sunlight. It was old but she kept it razor sharp and lightly coated in oil so that there wasn't even a fleck of rust on its blade.

Her upper body was protected by one thin woolen under-shirt, one woolen buttoned shirt, and a heavy mackinaw jacket. Her lower body was encased in wool long johns, and her head was warmed by a slouch hat. Her outer trousers were wool, secured with a thin, brown leather belt. There were good wool socks under her knee-high leather boots.

The sun shone brightly and eventually she stood and took off her soaking jacket and then her pants. Her skin was white and pale and covered in goose bumps, and she gnashed her teeth in convulsive shivers. She leaned forward and wretched water and bile until her chest ached. Her head spun and she gasped for air as she shivered and wept. She wobbled to her feet and started wringing her shirt in her numb hands.

"I could be gone in a day," she thought in a moment of fierce clarity. The wind gusted across her chest and she thought she felt colder than she ever could have imagined. Sharp crystals of snow stung her bare skin and her ears rung. Above her, thin grey clouds were stacked like cordwood but the sky was bright and hopeful.

Liana draped the wet shirt over her shoulders and slid her arms into soaked sleeves. Her shivering fingers were barely able to do up the buttons. With the same determination, she wrung out her jacket and slid on her pants and socks. When she was done she burst into tears. Her staccato sobs and gasps were swallowed by the lonely forest. She stepped backwards and leaned against the log, exhausted and frozen.

She was too tired to weep for long and slowly caught her breath and stopped shivering. She turned to gaze upstream at the end of the canyon. Its enormous granite walls dropped into the bedrock under the sandy beach that was buried under snow. From this vantage point, the bottom of the canyon resembled an enormous gate. Liana could see the spray from the hole but could not see any white or foam. The canoe halves were nowhere to be seen. The hole had digested Henry's canoe, and Liana felt an enormous sadness for its loss.

The island was not much bigger than a baseball diamond. It was narrow on both the upstream and downstream ends and wider in the middle. Even at its broadest width, it was less than five hundred feet across. The expanse was treeless, with a small ridge of sand and gravel in the centre almost like a spine. A driftwood log divided the island neatly from top to bottom. Its five-foot girth sported a halo of torn roots on one end and a jagged break on the other. Roots like a spread hand extended ten feet into the sky and in all directions. Rough bark had peeled off most of the log in large flakes and its trunk was now largely a smooth, silvery grey.

Liana considered her options. Swimming to shore seemed impossible; she would certainly drown or freeze. Besides, she was not a strong swimmer, and there wasn't a suitable log or fallen tree to use to float her to shore. But waiting on the island for the ice to span the gap—ice strong enough to support her weight—gave her little chance of survival either. The question that troubled Liana was how long the ice would take to freeze. She had lived in the North long enough to know that travel on frozen rivers could be fast and safe for a single person or even a loaded sled and team. But without food or fire, she knew that her odds of lasting long enough for freeze up were slim.

Liana studied the great forest that crowded the river and climbed the hills that formed her world. Dark spruce and pine were punctuated with the occasional grove of leafless aspen. The brilliant aspen leaves had already fallen, brightening the forest duff with yellow litter now mostly blanketed by snow. It was the kind of forest that Liana would have found beautiful under different circumstances. The forest now appeared menacing in its breathy silence.

Like a wedge, the island divided the river into two almost equal portions. The river purled sluggishly around the island, its glassy surface creased with thin pulls from the current. The current ran only a few miles an hour after it exited the canyon, spent from the miles of crashing turbulence. Along both shores was an irregular shelf of thin, clear ice. The ice rimming the shore appeared to have a greater mass than the ice forming on the island. The bitter cold of the river exiled her and she felt lucky to have washed onto the island, but she also knew she was trapped.

Liana remembered how comfortable she had been crouching in the hunting blind on the alpine plain and how the protection from the wind had been incredible. She walked to the sunny side of the log and examined it carefully. The wood rested on a bed of frozen sand and fine gravel. Liana rested on her haunches and started to shovel with her hands. She kicked her heels into the gravel when her hands became frozen and useless. After about twenty minutes she had dug a five-foot-long trench. Liana piled the excavated snow, sand, and gravel beside the log for later use. Liana then started the process of gathering rocks from the beach. She ripped the stones from the sand and staggered under their weight back to the log. Liana crafted a foundation with the largest stones along the perimeter of the excavation joined the log on both sides in a crude semi-circle. The cracks between the stones were carefully filled with the snow, sand, and gravel. She placed a thin layer of sand on top of this foundation and then piled another row of rocks on top of it to make a continuous wall. A third and fourth and fifth layer of stones and sand and gravel followed the second. Before dusk, Liana had built a lair using the log and wall of rock and filler. She marveled at her handiwork. This snuggery would protect her from the deep chill of night and the brisk winds and boldness of the days. It was her fortress against the cold and snows and she would feel protected behind its walls, nestled against the hundred-year-old log.

Exhausted, Liana lifted her leg to straddle the pony wall and stoop under the log. Once inside, she curled up in the shelter of the great log. It felt cool and damp and her wet clothes clung to her sallow frame. She braced for what she imagined would prove the longest night of her life.

Liana glanced at the darkening night sky through the entrance. A weak breeze rustled the bare trees and evergreens on the hillside. It took her back to the day she had met Henry for the first time. He was working for her father, clearing his claim at the top of Desmond Creek. Her father had brought Henry home for dinner, and he barely spoke during the entire meal.

When Henry had told Liana that it wasn't safe for her in town, she did not question him. She had few friends or acquaintances in Dawson City and knew that Henry was an honest man. She knew that many would never have approved of a young European girl living alone with a Native man, but Henry was so like a grandparent, Liana didn't find their arrangement awkward. After several days of hiking they arrived at Henry's little cabin. It hadn't been visited in years and her first impression of the two-bedroom shack was shock at its incredible stench. Henry had skinned animals inside the cabin and the smell of their rotting hides permeated the log walls long after the pelts had been sold. Henry knew skinning inside would offend but it was just the way things were. His arthritic hands would never have been able to handle the cold and he would risk damaging the furs with his scraper when he cleaned them. Henry was a practical man and his cabin resonated with these choices.

Henry was what many called "Old Indian," which meant he primarily lived traditionally. He ate simple foods, mostly meat and fish he caught or traded; he carried a pouch of herbs that he used to treat various infections and illnesses. He went to town infrequently and preferred to live on the land in a scattered array of small log cabins.

Liana knew that Henry's stories were her key to survival and she hoped she could remember enough of them. The cold settled evenly throughout her body and its heaviness left her feeling nauseated. It was a weight above her brows, across her chest, and behind her knees. The cold penetrated everywhere and she escaped its crushing burden only briefly by remembering happier times.

Liana climbed from her lair stiffly and faced the blankness of morning. The sun had climbed over the ridges but wasn't warm or comforting, but at least the tortuous night had ended. She was still damp and exhausted from the swim two days ago and the cold had settled into the pit of her stomach with a dull ache. She stood facing the river and the canyon far upstream and sighed.

The little island divided the steely northern river neatly in two. All around, the great forest, with the exception of the high mountain tops, spread as far as she could see. In contrast, the island was barren of vegetation. The only piece of wood was the enormous log and like everything else it was blanketed by a few inches of snow. The island was devoid of anything to eat, even grass. There wasn't any firewood, other than the enormous log. Sand, gravel, and a few sizable rocks ringing the water's edge were the sum total of her resources. She sat in the lee of the log and braced herself for another uncomfortable night.

Liana felt as though she was falling apart; each moment she was weaker than the next. No one knew where she was. All hope had perished with Henry in the ashes of their cabin. The small stone wall and trench she had built at the base of the log gave her some protection from the cold but didn't seem strong or warm enough. The cold was ravenous, gnawing on her energy like a big cat pouncing on a chunk of raw meat. Each day found her less alert and aware. Her bones ached so painfully that she had no wish to move. It would be so easy to doze, to sleep, to sleep forever.

A story Henry had told her played in Liana's head again and again. Of all Henry's stories, this was the one that Liana had come to hate since being washed onto the barren island. She wondered if it were based on a true story and assumed it was. The situation was very similar to her current plight. Henry told her the tale one afternoon as they stacked firewood. It was about a Cree woman stranded near a river with her children, slowly starving to death. In desperation, she cut herself for fish bait. She managed to catch a grayling and the family survived. Liana felt this was one of the few stories that Henry had told her that didn't seem mystical.

"Your stories in stories," thought Liana, gritting her teeth in frustration. "I don't understand them." But the problem with this story was that it seemed plausible to her, perhaps even probable. "Henry's people know how to survive," she thought. What terrified Liana most was that she knew what she must do. Lying under the log slowly starving and freezing was a horrible fate but using her own flesh as bait was unthinkable. "Will the ice ever reach me, or will I die here?" she muttered into the morning.

The soul-robbing quiet made her feel like the only living thing in the forest. Nothing ever seemed to move or make a noise in the frozen expanse. Liana pushed air from her chest to empty it and then inhaled an icy breath deep into her lungs. The day absorbed her sigh and the sound trailed to nothing. Liana felt more alone than ever. Once again she waited patiently for clarity.

She emptied her bladder quickly, hating to expose her naked backside to the cold air, and then raised her arms over her head and stretched until she felt more alert. She was as ready as she would ever be. Taking a deep breath, she reached her shaking right hand for the knife on her belt. With a deft motion she flipped its glinting blade open with one hand while lifting her jacket and shirts with her other hand. Her pale hip, coated with goose bumps, shivered in the bracing morning air. Liana grasped a pinch of skin and with an anticipatory wince fixed her gaze on the featureless sky. She hesitated momentarily and then drew the knife through her flesh. Dark blood rushed into the incision as if a dam had broken. A guttural moan escaped involuntarily from her throat and resonated through her clenched teeth. She twisted her head to examine the cut. Thin blood trickled through her fingers and onto the gravel of the frozen beach. She felt dizzy and closed her eyes.

Before she could think further or suffer the intensity of the fresh wound a second longer, she drew the knife across her hip a second time. A bloody ribbon of warm flesh the size of her little finger dropped into her hand. Liana dropped the knife and carefully placed the flesh on a flat rock. Then she lay on her back on the icy gravel nearby. Tears filled her eyes as she shuddered with the pain of her sacrifice. Her breath whispered rhythmically with her heartbeat. Somewhere nearby an enormous raven croaked a greeting to the rising sun and then the forest became still once more.

When her breathing slowed, Liana reached into a jacket pocket and removed a woolen sock. She pressed it gingerly against the wound and felt the wet warmth of blood fill the loose fibers. It was as close to a bandage as she could muster. In preparation for this morning, she had removed and washed the sock in the clear river two days earlier. Liana tried to remain still and pushed her hand against the wound to slow the bleeding. She breathed shallowly and continued lying on her back until the sun had climbed high into the sky. The thought of cutting her hip had tortured her, and she had spent the night sliding into nightmares and then starting awake with the dread of first light. Liana's head was starting to spin, and the incision throbbed as if it were twice its size.

She watched tenuous clouds blow into view over a snow-white mountain peak and felt the chill of the morning anew. The clouds seemed to stall overhead and Liana braced herself against the stillness. In her isolation, stillness had become a kind of invisible demon, threatening her to slip away without as much as a whisper in her dreams. She wished she had mastered whistling. She considered singing, despite the rawness of her throat.

A soft mist shrouded the river as the water split around the island and came together on the other side. The quiet settled into her bones with the cold and pain and hunger. "The quiet and cold are different sides of the same silver coin on this miserable island," she thought. She closed her eyes and rested for more than an hour in the meek sunshine.

Liana opened her eyes to scour the riverbank for wildlife, thinking she had heard something coming to the river to feed or drink. Her eyes restlessly scanned the waterline up and down, searching for the slightest motion. She saw only the trees swaying in the occasional breeze. "Where are the animals?" she wondered. "Am I just not seeing them? There should be river otters, at least." She wished she were still asleep and reluctantly acknowledged the throb from her hip.

She spent most days studying the forest closest to the island. But this particular morning, inexorably, her thoughts slipped back to the two moments when her blade sliced into her hip. She could feel the knife separating her flesh. As she held the sock against the wound, her mouth was dry and tasted bitter. The odds of surviving the island were remote, and Liana knew it.

She reached forward and picked up the knife she had dropped after cutting her hip. The blade was still bloody and she carefully wiped it clean on her pants and closed the blade. The knife had belonged to her father. It was made by Laguiole, the famous knife makers of Theirs, France. Her father had told her Napoleon himself had given Laguiole the right to make that particular form of knife because the men of the family had shown great courage in battle.

The knife was slim and elegant, with rosewood sides and brass bollards. An elegant bumblebee-shaped button was wrought to unlock the blade. With only gentle pressure from her thumb, Liana could easily depress the button. Her father had made a moose-hide sheath with a matching rawhide lanyard that dangled from the knife. It was the only object belonging to her father that Liana still had. She treasured it.

When her father had been found, the Mounties had kept the knife in their barracks for Liana to collect. His body had been found tangled in a logjam in the creek bordering his mining claim. The Mounties assumed her dad had slipped into the river and been swept beneath the logs by the current. When the cart carrying his body shrouded in a dirty horse blanket reached town, Liana dropped to her knees in grief. First her mother, and now her father was gone.

Henry had reached down, picked her up, and taken her back to her cabin. He told her that it wasn't safe for her to stay, and in her confused state Liana didn't question him. Henry was a trusted friend of her father and the only person willing to involve himself in the new orphan's affairs. They spent the evening loading up all her essentials and carrying them to a cache outside the town. After her father was laid to rest the next day, Liana and Henry quietly left town without anyone noticing.

As before, Liana's ears pricked with the sound of voices from across the river. A soft shout that sounded like someone saying "porch step" echoed from a source unseen. Breathlessly, Liana searched the north side of the river. She tilted her head to better hear another cry. And then she heard it again: "porch step." She scrambled to her feet and took a couple of steps in the direction of the sound. Then she turned her head and waited for the person to say something again or step from the shadow of the forest onto a nearby beach. She waited patiently but when the silence persisted Liana cupped her hands around her mouth. "Hello," she screamed. "I'm over here. I need help!"

Holding her breath, she waited for a reply. When there was no sound, she screamed "Hello" once more, excitedly this time. Liana stood still and waited for a response but only the forest rustled in the gentle breeze. "Hello!" she screamed half a dozen times more. She waited for a response that would not come. Liana knew that the forest could play tricks but this call had seemed so clear, so human, so promising.

She wondered why someone would yell "porch step"? It made no sense. It must be the wind in the trees, she told herself, still scanning the forest for someone to appear. Who would have said something so ridiculous, anyway? Facing the direction from which the sound had come, she sat on the beach holding the wound hoping that she was wrong and someone would miraculously appear. Eventually Liana retreated to the log and waited. "Am I being watched?" she wondered. "Am I truly alone?"

Her fingertips tingled despite the fact she had slept all night with her hands in her armpits or between her legs. Her left foot felt like she had a stone inside her boot, but she knew she didn't. Every morning this foot protested painfully, and when she went outside, the limb would throb for a few moments with the increased circulation. Liana couldn't remember injuring her foot and assumed something must have sprained or bruised it as she was helplessly washed downstream.

Liana felt marooned in the weak afternoon light, watching the river's quiet parade and the wind in the trees. She had survived many nights. Aside from the intense sharpness of this morning's wound and her chilled extremities, she was weak but fine and she consoled herself with this knowledge. She knew it would take hours of soaking in the sun before she felt less cold, but on the island she would never feel warm. She decided that it made more sense to rest under the log, and so she climbed into her lair. The wound had clotted, but when she shifted her weight or moved it would open and trickle blood. She was prepared to spend the day under the log holding the cut, and she pulled her hat down over her ears and raised her legs onto the stone wall. Liana feared infection and the wound hurt far more than she anticipated so she made herself comfortable and spent the day resting.

For the thousandth time, Liana examined the short wall she had built and the gaps it made where it joined the log. "If I could fill the gaps, it would be much warmer," she thought. But the island offered no moss, leaves, or anything else she could think of to act as insulation. Liana thought about the gaps and the way the light shone through the openings. The light itself seemed to harbour gusts of cold. Most of the damp sand she had used to fill the gaps had frozen and already fallen away. Sharp drafts penetrated the gloom. The island that had saved her days before now seemed intent to exile her.

Liana once again pulled the knife from its sheath and raised it to the light. Its blade glinted in the sun and she thought about her father. She examined the elaborate engraved filigree along the back of the blade and the odd bumblebee locking mechanism. Napoleon's golden bee seemed out of place in this desolate spot. "What would Papa think of this?" she asked herself.

Liana coveted this knife, her only connection to her family, and a quick passage to so many memories. It was only a simple Laguiole folding knife, the kind one could purchase at almost any outfitters' shop in France. This simple little knife now held her fate and Liana was grateful to have it on her waist. She turned and in the shadowy gloom she studied the bloody bit of flesh on the rock. It was white and coated in dried blood. The sun almost reached the log and Liana closed her eyes and rested. Her breath was laboured and her wounded hip was pounding and sore. She pressed the honey-bee, slowly folded the blade, and slid the gleaming knife back into its sheath.

The raven's throaty song filled the gloom. "Ravens aren't anything like magpies," thought Liana. Magpies are always in search of the next shiny object to add to their stores. Magpies collect anything twinkling and bright and painstakingly knit tinsel into the sticks and grasses of their nests. "Even when ravens eat garbage they seem stately," she thought. Liana smiled as she remembered the cleverness of a constable stealing dog food. A single raven bounced near the bowl to taunt the dog, and when he chased the annoying bird several others would swoop down for a meal. "Ravens create opportunities. They're clever," she thought.

Liana thought about the events that had landed her on the little island. The improbability of her surviving this series of events animated her. She felt lucky and damned at the same time. She considered this thought throughout the day with frustration and awe. There seemed only one way for her to escape the island, and it was a long shot at best.

The little island and her impossibly long wait bored her. A good book would be almost more welcome than a juicy steak dinner. She stared distantly into the forest, scrutinizing its subtleties. She gazed at the gravel and sand and considered the possibilities of where it had originated. The glassy black rocks must be from a volcano, she thought, and she turned her eyes up at the hills to search for a caldera that did not exist, at least not within sight of the island. Aside from the massive stranded log, there were only rocks and sand and gravel on the island. Liana's hands craved holding something that wasn't a mineral.

Rarely did she allow herself to think about food, as the mere thought made her hunger all the more agonizing. Instead she tried to think about the people and places she knew. She tried to remember the words of songs. Sometimes she thought of Henry. Often she thought about her parents, particularly her father. She thought about what he would think if he knew she had cut herself with his knife—the knife he had said resembled her mother in its beauty and elegance.

Liana lay under the log, crouched in her lair. She looked at its silvery surface in close detail. The log was at least a hundred years old. It was missing most of its bark and all of its branches, except for one thick stub of an arm at the top of the log. One day it would be washed off the island in a flood. The log would bob and roll in the current, swept downstream for hundreds of miles. Rocks and branches would stretch out their tentacles to claw at it, delay it. If it didn't get hung up on another gravel bar or in a logjam by the time it reached the sea, only a few splinters of wood would remain. Liana touched the log and felt its weathered grey sheen. She closed her eyes and rested for what felt like a long time. When she reopened them the sun was hidden behind dark clouds. The grim sky lit the forest in a sullen monochrome. The pine and spruce trees were cloaked in a dark, lifeless hue. Leafless willow and birch crowded the river on both sides. The flat light was so dim it could not produce a single shadow.

Beneath the log, Liana felt snuggled up to a silent sister, buffered from the harshness of the island. At eighteen, Liana was a compact figure, not very tall and with a slight build. Her light brown hair was wiry and usually worn in a single braid. Despite her father's opinion of her, she felt she had plain features. Although she was lean and fit from years of active living, her hands bore no calluses. She could hike endlessly without tiring and could climb a tree as quickly as a squirrel.

Liana loved walking and reading Wordsworth, Emerson, and Thoreau. Her favorite poem was "I Wandered Lonely as a Cloud." Liana liked Wordsworth's idea that everything was connected. It was reassuring. Besides, daffodils were her favorite flower. But Liana thought about Wordsworth little these days. The sublime didn't exist on this cheerless island. Instead, Liana knew her survival depended on rational decisions and luck.

When she wasn't floating in her dreams or soundlessly moving her lips to the words of the poems and songs she knew, Liana considered her escape from the island. Escape was a thought that was never far away. And this day while leaning on her hand over the wound to stop the bleeding, the thought of escape filled her. She was optimistic that her luck would change and that opportunity would present itself. She imagined the ice spanning the gap between the island and the shore and carefully stepping across a frozen crystal bridge. Once on the shore she would follow the river downstream to town.

The day had never awakened, though Liana felt more alive than she had in days. The knife had proved to her that she was alive. The pain of slicing her flesh resonated through her soul. She felt the horrible intensity of the knife cutting through her delicate skin. She felt a charge of energy from the glint of steel as it crossed her hip twice. It was a grim thought, but one that woke her up and invigorated her. She had hatched a plan and had carried it out without wavering. "Henry should be proud," she thought.

Liana dreamed of being able to hibernate just long enough to awaken to the river already frozen. She would rise in the twilight and slowly trudge through the snow, over the thickened ice and away from the barren island. If she could conserve her energy, slow her breathing and her heart, she could wake in a few weeks when the ice bridged the gap. Liana huddled deep into her jacket and pulled her legs up close to her chest. She held the sock hard against the wound. It would take all day and most of the night for the cut to fully clot.

Liana slept fitfully but with greater hope. Taking action made her feel strong. Many times during the night Liana craned her neck and peered out from under the log at the night sky, excited that she would soon be fishing. The clouds of stars and intense blackness of the night made her feel small and forgotten. Liana watched the bright constellations of Pegasus, Leo, and Orion track across the sky. The day would slowly reveal itself. The sun, a muted orange hint, would light the sky before climbing over the silhouette of mountains. The chrysanthemum brightness filled her with optimism.

The days were now shorter and only a brief reprise from the monotony of the dark. Like the other days, the orange would quickly fade and the sky would return to its usual colourless steel grey for the rest of the day. A gentle breeze would add a sting to the crispness of morning and increase her misery. Liana waited beneath the log for the air to warm, but it never did. A thick mist hovered over the river and Liana could not see the forest at all. But she knew that the ice shelf was growing; she trusted the depth of the cold and its power to make a path for her.

The raven was getting used to her presence. The big bird now sat on the opposite end of the log on the highest shaft of a frost-covered root. Its perch was no more than fifteen feet above the beach and was by far the highest point on the island. From this vantage, the raven could scour the entire island with its mysterious eyes. It was the same raven that had shrieked when Liana cut herself, she was sure. To Liana, the big bird looked sinister.

The raven shifted its weight from one leg to the other and preened its enormous wings. It was aware of Liana's every move, though it didn't always seem to be watching. There was intelligence in this bird, and Liana didn't like the way it studied her. She searched its dark eyes and its dark, sharp, spear-shaped beak. At least song birds made wonderful calls, and water birds were enjoyable to watch. But the slyness of ravens always unsettled her. Liana thought that ravens always seemed unprepared for the North. Somehow, their featherless feet did not freeze in the deep cold. Their cartoonish calls and their communal flocks were always boisterous and loud.

The first time she saw a raven, Liana was shocked by its size. She couldn't believe it was bigger than a chicken and still able to fly. Ravens were brave enough to torment bald eagles and many times she had seen them in pursuit. It was during the summer when eagles became restless, waiting for the spawning salmon to choke the rivers and creeks in their multitudes. A group of four or five ravens seemed to enjoy ganging up on a single eagle, pecking at its tail feathers to elicit screeching cries.

The island's raven broke the silence with a long croak that resonated through the forest. It made sounds no animal should be able to make. Deep, guttural escapes of air mixed with rhythmic screeches and pops. Ravens could sound like a church bell or a lost kitten. In Liana's weakened state, the raven's calls were surreal and intimidating. She winced every time it sounded. Liana looked up at the raven's perch on the uppermost root of the log and the raven gurgled its ethereal song.

Liana despised this bird. She had seen flocks of ravens screeching and fighting over the eyes of dead moose and caribou. Ravens were the vultures of the North. Liana knew this raven sat on its perch so that another raven wouldn't claim Liana for itself. It wasn't that it was merely waiting for an opportunity; the raven was greedily guarding its prize. "You're not getting my eyes," she promised the brooding bird. Liana felt the sharpness of the wound on her hip when she spoke. The raven tilted its head and shot a glance at Liana and then continued its preening in earnest. The raven had the luxury of time, which Liana did not. It knew winter was coming and Liana wouldn't last.

In the soft light under the log, Liana took the frozen piece of bait and warmed it in her hand until it was soft and pliable. She slowly fed it onto a small fishhook she kept for emergencies in a leather slip in the front pocket of her jacket. Her fingertips turned red from the thawed blood. She unwound the short piece of fishing line attached to the hook and checked the knot. Her motions were slow and deliberate. Her fingers were stiff. She had no energy to waste and much to lose. Her preparations had to be perfect.

When the hook was ready, she carefully positioned herself to climb out from under the log without disturbing the snow on the stone pony-wall. As she stretched her stiffened legs and bent her torso to squirm out, she could feel her wound start to bleed. A small trickle of blood seeped from her hip as she stumbled across the ice and snow that covered the rocky beach. The rocks glistened with a coating of ice and appeared wet with the thin glaze. The sun was bright and Liana squinted at the sparkling snow and hardpan of the island.

She strode determinedly to the downstream end of the island where there was an eddy in the river. The water was clear and copper coloured and she could see to the rocky, weedless bottom. At its deepest, the river was six feet in this pool. "Perfect for grayling," she thought. Liana thought the grayling's enormous dorsal fin and light blue-green colouring beautiful. To her they almost looked like they could fly. She tossed the bait and hook beyond the ice shelf into the weak current. With a gentle plunk, the bait broke the glassy surface and slowly sank. Inches before it hit the bottom, she tugged on the line, fearing a snag. Liana stumbled backwards and brushed a thin layer of snow from a boulder facing the river, the sun at her back. After she settled herself on the boulder, she pulled her hat down to her brow and prepared to wait, optimistic that her suffering wasn't in vain and soon she would have a fish.

Liana knew that the salmon had finished spawning many weeks before she washed onto the island. Salmon camps had lined the Yukon River with their nets strung along booms made of spruce logs. Fish wheels modeled on Scandinavian originals fifty feet high had slowly spun in the current, scooping salmon night and day. Massive log drying racks with bright orange salmon split down the middle squatted in the last rays of summer. Her hope was for a straggler, a salmon that was sick or weak or somehow delayed in reaching its spawning grounds. It was a big river and had to have a lot of fish in it, she thought. If not a salmon, perhaps a Dolly Varden would find her bait. Most likely, a scrawny grayling would find its way onto the hook and in an instant be on shore cut into a hundred bite-sized pieces. Liana feared weakening and drifting away in her sleep, her body washed into the river with the spring floods. She could almost feel the raven's sharp beak pulling out her eyes, leaving grotesque, empty sockets in its wake.

Aside from the faint hum of the distant canyon and the gentle rustle of the breeze, the day was silent. Liana glanced upstream at the sentinel rock wall and thought of the horror of the rapids it contained. She wished that she had been more alert and hadn't entered the canyon. A portage would have taken a day or two but would have assured her safety.

She pressed her wound with one hand and tucked her chin into her jacket. Hours passed and her hip burned. Flurries of snow buffeted her face and made her squint and her cheek muscles tired. Liana kept her vigil but could not see any fish. She preferred the shelter of the friendly log. Crouching next to the river left her exposed to the breeze. But catching fish could easily tip the scales of survival in her favour and help her escape this miserable place.

As the sun plunged behind the ridge Liana listlessly pulled in the line. She wound the line and carefully placed it, the hook, and the pale white bait in the leather slip and into her chest pocket. She looked into the current and searched once more for the telltale flash of a fish. She dipped her hand into the river and cupped a couple of slurps of water. It trickled down her parched throat and she felt momentarily revived, but hunger pulsed in her belly and her hip throbbed. She stood stiffly and raised her hands over her head and stretched her aching back. In the fading light she lifted her face to the brightening stars and closed her eyes. At the end of this fruit-less day, Liana felt more discouraged than she had ever felt before in her life. She looked at the log in the shadowy gloom and her heart sank as she struggled with the reality of another tortuous night.

Liana scanned the great forest and its utter desolation star-tled her. The vastness of the dusk sky washed over her, and faint stars dotted the indigo sky. She turned and stumbled in the twilight back toward the log. As she climbed under it, the raven twisted its head and called its dreadful song one last time. She could see its throat expand and contract as the greasy notes slid from its distended beak. As Liana slid her legs underneath the log, she said in a defiant whisper "Not today." As if he understood, the raven fell quiet and preened its wings in the fading light. A heavy veil of cold slipped down the mountainsides and poured into the valley.

In Liana's dreams the raven perched on a polished walnut armoire in her childhood bedroom. The raven tried to steal her silver hairbrush but it had difficulty picking it up and was unable to fly out her bedroom window. Instead it flapped around her room, knocking dolls and books from their shelves. Liana caught a framed photograph of her grandmother before it hit the floor. Wolves bared their teeth from the open window. Liana tried to shoo the raven out her window by waving her hands and shouting. Instead, the raven flew into her closet where it started shredding her Sunday dress with its dagger-sharp beak. The wolves howled. Liana lay on her bed and covered her ears and closed her eyes until the raven stopped its rampage and the wolves wandered away.

The next morning sunlight pierced the entrance of Liana's chamber beneath the log. She lifted her shirts and jacket to check the cut. Despite being red and angry, it was starting to heal. Liana was surprised the wound was looking so good. She prodded gently on the skin around the cut and felt its sharpness. Reassured, Liana pushed her tangled hair off her forehead and carefully climbed out from beneath the log without disturbing the snow covering the pony wall. In the brightness she was surprised by how much the island had changed. In the last week it had gained almost a foot of snow. In the distance Liana could see that the ice shelf had grown as well.

Liana had come to yearn for morning, when she would fill her belly with water. It felt good to feel the sensation of fullness, even if it was only water. Her mouth frequently salivated and often she thought of hunger, her constant companion, for uninterrupted hours. Like a campfire left to burn down in the night, Liana could feel her essence begin to fade. She thought about herself as mere embers and hoped when the opportunity to escape arose she would have the strength to resurrect herself.

She held the leather slip with the frozen bait, hook, and line like a treasure. There was no turning back. She thought that she shouldn't let her bad luck of the previous day discourage her. She once again took up her silent fishing vigil like a young novitiate assigned to pray continuously. Weakening, her muscles growing slack, her waistband growing loose, Liana was clumsier each day she remained on the island. She pulled her arm back and tossed the line into the silent current. It made a small plunk and then the transparent line sank into the eddy until it was hidden under the ice shelf. The line wasn't long enough for her to sit on the rocks. Instead she crouched on the ice with an arm outstretched toward the river. She wondered if she was alert and strong enough to pull in a fish if she hooked one.

She threw the rig into the river and then jigged the hook, moving the line back and forth around the eddy before letting it sit on the bottom. Hours passed to no avail. She didn't even see a fish, let alone feel one at the end of her line. Before long the sun had climbed high in the sky. Much of the morning chill was gradually burned away by the weak warmth of the sun.

"Where are the fish?" she asked aloud. She had seen salmon in other rivers choking the current and turning the river crimson red with their rotting carcasses. The hook-like beaks of the disintegrating sockeye broke the surface as they crowded eddies and rested before charging the current. She would give anything to have just one salmon now—a single, half dead, molting salmon.

When she was a child, Liana's father would take her trout fishing on a muddy tributary of the Seine. He was a good fisherman and their wicker basket was often filled with writhing trout after just a short while on the water. She was startled the first time she saw languid sockeye salmon choking the entrance of a creek near Dawson City. She had never seen so many fish in one place. The abundance she had known stood in stark contrast to her present reality.

Liana cupped her hand over her eyebrows to cut the glare of the water and ice. She scanned the river's surface for the darting of a fish. She stared into the deep pool and concentrated her attention on a single spot in front of a large rock. The rock was dark and Liana felt that a silvery fish would be easier to see when it swam in front of the rock. She spent hours concentrating on this minute area of the river but never saw anything. It was as though the river didn't have fish, but Liana knew that was not possible. "All rivers have fish," she said under her breath. "How can a river suddenly be barren?"

The raven sat on its perch on the root of the log, feigning disinterest. It preened its wings, oblivious to Liana's struggle. It didn't make a sound. The raven didn't even call to her anymore. Liana felt listless and beaten.

Liana's thoughts drifted beyond the island and back in time. She remembered once seeing gypsy "fish ticklers" in a village outside Paris. Her parents had taken her on a picnic and the train ride had been exciting as they stood outside between the coach cars. Brightly dressed gypsies were camped in their caravans next to a muddy little creek. A lone gypsy man sat next to the river with his arm submerged past his elbow. He wore a purple bandana that set off his wiry black beard and exotic dark eyes. Liana and her parents stood next to a tree and watched the bent man. Her father told her that the man was a tickler, one who could catch trout with only his bare hands. He wiggled his fingers and the curious trout swam close to them. Somehow the gypsy would end up stroking the trout's chin or belly. Once the trout became less timid, they moved within his grasp. In an instant the fish tickler grabbed a trout firmly and hauled it onto the bank, all in a single motion. He dropped it in the long grasses next to the river and let it flop around. The old gypsy grinned at Liana and her family.

This memory moved her to action. Impulsively, Liana pushed up her sleeves and stepped forward onto the ice shelf. Excitedly she reached toward the river with her arm. Realizing her mistake, Liana pulled her shirt and jacket down over her wrist. "The mind plays tricks," she mumbled softly, and carefully stepped backwards, startled by her momentary lapse of judgment.

Liana had heard stories of people who had frozen to death. Everyone in the North knew stories of how the winter had taken the unprepared or unlucky, how hypothermia so confused its victims that they had became mad and thought they were burning up but were freezing instead. In their delusions, they would rip off their clothing and writhe naked in snowdrifts, their movements growing slower and slower. The deep arctic cold would swallow them up and they would be found twisted like deformed statues with horrific gasping expressions. Liana feared that, as she weakened, she would meet a similar end. Already she had almost tried fish tickling. "I must keep away from the river until it's frozen," she told herself.

Liana's pants were feeling loose. She inspected her belt and decided to carve another hole so she didn't have to hold them up. Liana wrapped the free end of the fishing line around her ankle and then undid her belt buckle and pulled the leather tail until it was free. She then took out her knife and, using the point of the blade, swiveled it until she punctured the leather with a tiny hole. Liana then slid the belt back through the loops and did up the buckle at the new hole. With a sense of satisfaction, she settled back into the cold gravel.

The ice was gradually closing the gap between the shore and the island, especially on the east side where the current was less strong. As the river froze, its current lost its energy. Imperceptibly it slowed and soon only a trickle of water would gurgle through the deepest of its channels under layers of ice. In places, the ice would be more than six feet thick. But now it was only a thin layer extending thirty feet from shore and less than fifteen feet from the island.

Liana tried not to think about fishing. She felt it was bad luck to be overly eager for anything and she didn't want to jinx herself. But her thoughts continually returned to the river and her inability to attract even the most inconsequential of fish. After half an hour, her arm was stiff and bloodless and her legs cramped. She stood and stretched her legs and lowered her arm while looking across the river at the forest. "How am I going to walk off this island?" she thought. "I'm falling apart and soon I won't be even able to walk."

Sitting beside the river fishing felt more lonely than slumbering under the log. Fishing left too much time to explore her darker thoughts. Under the log she entered a dreamy twilight where she could escape the island in her dreams. Fishing was depressing and the raven was always waiting, reminding her of the odds of surviving the island. She looked at the river stirring in the gap and found the dappled ripples of the surface hypnotic.

Liana turned and stumbled through the ankle-deep snow to her shelter. As she climbed under the log she heard the unmistakable flapping of the raven's wings. She turned to watch her tormentor disappearing downriver. Its outstretched black wings beating powerfully as it climbed above the largest spruce trees bordering the water. Liana watched the raven slowly fade into the distance and felt immense envy at its ability to fly away. As it flew, it called its grotesque song, the croaking and groans gradually becoming softer and fading into silence.

Liana was glad to see the raven fly away, but despite her dislike for the bird, she felt more alone than ever. She took a deep breath and looked at the distant forest before climbing under the log. With a sigh, Liana curled into the frozen gravel and closed her eyes. She braced for the frigid night. Another day had passed.

Liana's eyes opened bit by bit. They felt gritty and her vision was blurred. Another morning.

Without getting to her feet, Liana lifted her shirts and jacket to check the cut on her hip. Her wound throbbed and itched, which she felt was a good sign of healing. She lay under the log and leaned into the watery sunlight that pierced the entrance to her chamber and tried to focus a beam squarely on the incision. The wound was red and angry but was starting to heal, which surprised Liana under the circumstances. She pushed on the skin around the cut and it pleased her that it seemed to be less sensitive to pressure.

Liana pushed her matted auburn hair back from her forehead and braced for the reality outside of her shelter. Greasy tresses framed her gaunt, expressionless face. She carefully climbed out from beneath the log without disturbing the snow covering the pony wall. The more snow that accumulated on the wall, the warmer she felt at night. Once she was standing, the chill shrouded her like a heavy, restrictive cloak.

The raven had returned. He clutched his perch on the root of the log feigning disinterest, while listening attentively to every word Liana spoke. Occasionally he preened his wing feathers, or pecked his jet-black beak at small imperfections or dirt. He watched Liana indirectly out of boredom. They were locked in a contest of stamina to see whose will was stronger. This tension motivated her to persevere with fishing and survive until the river froze into a temporary bridge.

To throw the baited hook into the river, Liana now had to walk several feet onto the ice rim around the island. The ice was thin in places and Liana had to move carefully with short, gentle steps. She followed her footprints from previous mornings but the new snowfall made it more difficult for her to reach the fishing spot. Liana was clumsier and weaker, less alert and more uncoordinated, each day she remained on the island. She stumbled through the drifts with a slight stagger.

Liana pulled her arm back and tossed the line into the sluggish current. It made a glint as it broke the glassy surface of the water and she watched the line sink into the eddy until it was hidden under the ice shelf. Silent and alert, she waited. The sun slowly tracked across the sky and the day passed as so many had with a mixture of disappointment and boredom.

As sunset began to light the sky, Liana started to wind the line around her bare hand. After a few wraps, she gasped in disbelief. "The bait's gone!" she whispered. As she inched forward a few steps, the ice cracked along several penetrating faults. Instinctively, Liana froze and held her breath. She stepped toward the river to retrieve the bait but she couldn't even see it. She knew that the pool was only about six feet deep and that the bait likely hadn't drifted too far before sinking to the bottom. But none of this mattered. The cold would take her in only a few minutes.

Liana's mind raced with the necessity of retrieving the bait, and she started looking for an easy place to enter the river. "Don't do it," a voice inside her pleaded. "You'll freeze for sure." Liana stumbled backwards and stared with bewilderment at the river. Lumpy tears welled in her eyes. She felt as though she couldn't trust herself and feared that she would dive into the river despite the risk. She was losing control of her good judgment and this frightened her more than anything else had since the day Henry was shot.

Disheartened, Liana trudged back to where she had been fishing and fell onto a rock. She was flushed; tears ran down her grimy cheeks. Her heart sank as she examined the bare metal hook, and a ratcheting cry reverberated in her throat. Liana felt dizzy and squatted back on the rock. She looked away from the river and stared at the conformity of the snow. All her hopes had rested on catching fish. She couldn't return to the log empty-handed to slowly starve and freeze to death.

After several minutes Liana started to feel relief. "Almost a week of fishing," she told herself, "and I haven't even seen a single fish." She knew it was time to stop fishing and conserve her energy. Standing next to the river had brought her to delirium on several occasions. She had forced herself to stay exposed to the wind and cold, but now she could rest under the log and wait.

Liana glanced at the silhouette of the trees bordering the river. Henry had often told her, "My people are in the Jack pine roots." Liana looked at the forest and asked plaintively, "Are you there, Henry?" She dug her hands into her pockets and staggered away from the river.

Back at the log, Liana shuddered in the dank familiarity of her den. All she had to do now was last long enough for the ice to harden. She looked up at the sky and took a deep breath and considered her singular option. The river would freeze and she would escape to the shore and walk to town. She closed her eyes but sleep eluded her. The cold filled the valley with a shocking ferocity.

In the twilight of early morning, Liana heard the sound of snow falling. A hush filled the island and she could barely hear the whisper of the river. She was grateful that days were so brief this time of the year. Snow accumulated on the pony wall and the cave darkened as snow narrowed the entrance to a thin slit. The wind swirled a cornice of snow over the log, and ice granules seeped beneath it. Liana pushed the snow away from her lair so that she had enough room. Touching snow would melt it and make her wetter and even colder.

In the afternoon, when the sun felt like it was high in the sky, Liana finally decided to venture into the storm and break the monotony of her restless slumber. She carefully climbed out of the cavern. It felt much colder in the stark, gusty storm. Standing outside, Liana stretched her arms toward the sky. She closed her eyes and stuck out her tongue. It had never occurred to her that falling snow had a smell. Her tracks from the previous day had been buried, but this was fine, Liana thought, because the paths never led anywhere good. She walked toward the river to get a mouthful of water. She felt off-balance, disoriented by the snow and how the island and forest had so quickly been transformed.

Like everyone in the North, Liana knew that even during winter she needed to get at least one drink of water each day. Dehydration would kill her faster than hunger. As such, she followed a daily ritual of checking the progress of the ice and having at least a gulp of water. This day she ventured through the fresh snow to the jagged edge of the ice. The deep snow made her legs tingle as it fell over the cuff and into her boot. She followed the short trail to the ice and took a couple steps. It yielded slightly, cracking and popping under her weight.

She knelt near the edge of the ice and dunked her cupped hands into the meek current. She needed only a single palm full of water to feel satisfied but forced herself to take three.

The water trickled down her raw throat to her empty stomach. She felt indifferent to everything, not just the cold. She was startled by her reflection in the water. Her emaciated face was unfamiliar and frightening. She trudged back to the log and climbed underneath.

The storm raged through the evening and most of the night. Since she was always awake, she listened attentively to it surge and abate. She heard the shrill shriek of the storm and tingled with each gust that sent tendrils of drafts into the cave. Liana knew the river was slowing and losing energy; she could feel it.

Morning took forever to come. The snowfall had insulated the log, and Liana felt less cold, as if she had a light blanket covering her. Or perhaps she was dreaming this feeling of relative warmth, she thought, unsure of her own judgment.

Liana reminisced about Henry. She never knew when he would tell one of his stories: when he was cooking dinner, sitting beside the woodstove, stacking firewood outside. Sometimes he would tell several stories in a day, and other times, he wouldn't tell a story for weeks. Some were mystical stories about animal helpers; others were practical stories about not being selfish or the importance of talking gently to people. Once he told her about the first time he cooked dried beans. He had met some white prospectors on his trap line. They invited him into camp and traded him some meat for a pouch of tobacco. They were both fat and were new to living on the land. They offered Henry some beans from a large pot that bubbled on their fire. He ate three big bowls of beans, surprised by their sweetness and soft texture. It was a flavour he had never known, and he was hooked.

When Henry got to town he went to the general store and bought a bag of beans. Back at his cabin, his kids and wife watched him pour the beans into the pot of water on their woodstove and they eagerly waited for them to cook. He expounded on their incredible taste. His kids dogged him every five minutes and begged, "Are they done yet?" The men had told him to let the beans simmer in the water for at least a couple of hours, but Henry couldn't wait. After a half hour of boiling, he tasted a bean. It was black and hard and the water tasted foul. He let the beans cook for another hour and tasted them again, but they were still hard and bitter and not at all like the beans the prospectors had made. He let the beans cook the rest of the day and late into the next, but the beans never softened and the family was sullen. Disappointed, Henry took the beans outside and dumped the mess into the snow.

Later that year, he ran into those same trappers and he told them what had happened. They listened to his story with amusement and then howled with laughter. They explained that Henry had bought coffee beans. Henry also thought this was funny. "I'm a bush Indian," he said. "I never knew about coffee." Liana loved this story and the way Henry always easily laughed at himself.

Hours later she looked through the much smaller opening to see if it was still snowing. She saw stars and the emerald green of the northern lights. The narrow band of iridescence tore across the inky sky, swaying from side to side like a dancer. It was a sight Liana had never tired of. The northern lights had fascinated her more nights than she could remember. She watched them until most of the night had passed. Liana waited in the dark for daylight, dreaming and feeling strangely peaceful.

Liana awakened from her vigil to the faint call of the raven. At first she thought it must be her imagination and she lay motionless, listening attentively. She assumed that the raven had finally given up and left her alone. But the raven repeatedly cawed its horrible call, which became louder as it approached the island.

"He must be at least mile away," thought Liana as she sat up by leaning on her elbows. She peered into the morning twilight through the narrow slit. A heavy mist hung over the river and shrouded the island. The fog made it impossible for Liana to see a hundred feet. Everything looked different because of the fog and the fresh snow. Liana couldn't see the sun but it seemed to be mid-morning since the brightest patch of cloud was above the ridge. She scurried out from under the log. The snow rose past her knees. The fog was so dense she could barely see the shore on the other side of the river. The raven croaked its songs as it progressed ever closer. It was belching harsh music that Liana didn't recognize.

"Maybe it's a different raven?" she considered.

Liana imagined that the raven was flying from tree to tree, pausing to make its calls. But in the fog it was difficult to say just how far away he was. The fog and snow made distances and outlines less precise. Sound carried in the frozen forest and Liana knew to distrust her senses.

"Winter can play tricks on you," she reassured herself.

She tried to hone in on the raven's horrible song and looked in vain in every direction. And then she heard panting. Her heart stopped. It sounded close. In horror Liana scurried back under the log. She heard the panting again, deep and heavy. "Can ravens pant?" she asked herself, her heart racing.

An instant later Liana heard the unmistakable howl of a wolf. The piercing wails reverberated through the valley. It was the loudest sound Liana had heard in a long time; she braced against it and winced. The raven's persistent caw was provoking the wolf. The howls pierced the fog and cut through her like a hot knife through butter. When the howl finally stopped, the raven bubbled strange squeaks and excited pops. Liana thought she had heard every sound the raven was capable of making, but these rough cries were new to her. She heard the raven's wings flap as it came closer to the island. A moment later, the raven's bubbling songs were followed by the cacophony of an entire howling pack. The wolves shrieked in unison, their cries building in intensity. Desperately, Liana clutched her hands over her ears and cowered. She was suddenly stunned by the realization that the raven had led the wolves to the island.

"The raven has done this!" shrieked a terrified Liana. "The wolves are here to finish me off," she exclaimed. Liana closed her eyes. The wolves' shrieks blared like a freight train through her head.

Liana remained in the shadowy recesses of the log and hid from the raven and the wolves. Her heart raced and her ears throbbed from the commotion. Eventually she heard the rhythmic flapping of the raven's wings as it regained its perch on the log to croak its morbid songs gleefully. The wolves howled and yelped nearby. To Liana it sounded like an enormous pack—perhaps fifty or sixty strong. She knew that even a few wolves could sound like a pack but this group sounded genuinely enormous. She drew her knife from its sheath and held it with both hands. "They're close," panicked Liana. She waited in stillness and wondered why the wolves hadn't discovered her lair under the log. It was excruciating to have the raven and wolves united in a single, animated chorus.

Liana endured the howls for several minutes and gradually came to recognize one wolfish voice above the rest. It had a lower tone and its howls were shorter in duration; when it howled, all the other wolves did not join in unison. She knew that it must be the pack leader, an older male.

She curled into a ball and didn't look outside. She knew she couldn't be seen, but the wolves had her scent. And besides, the raven—her informant—knew where she lay. The howling seemed to come from the right bank, but because of the echo it felt like they had her surrounded. Liana braced for them to dive through the snow at any time and pull her into the fog. "They must be on the island already," she thought as she listened to the panting and sporadic yelps drawing ever nearer. The raven responded with its gruesome call, as if to warn, "Her eyes are mine!"

Eventually Liana opened her eyes and lifted her head to the opening between the snow and the log. Peering into the mist, she could just make out the dim outlines of the wolves on the opposite shore. They were dark with white and grey muzzles. Their massive haunches made them look powerful and menacing. She had never seen a live wolf before coming to the North, though she had seen their pelts many times. Stretched and dried, the skins always seemed exotic. She marveled at the thickness of the fur with outer hairs sometimes five inches long and a softer inner layer. The hair made the best parka ruffs, shedding snow like a steep roof.

"The wolves aren't on the island," she realized, consoling herself. "They can't get here." She was so relieved that she repeated to herself in disbelief, "They can't get here." Liana took a deep breath and settled back into the shadows. The wolves' panting was loud and heavy, but it was the jarring howls of the pack that filled her heart with terror.

The raven repeatedly called to the wolves with screeching gurgles and abrupt pops. The wolves had Liana's scent and knew that she cowered under the log. They were whipped into a frenzy. Liana waited breathlessly. Oh, how they wanted her! The diabolical raven encouraged them to swim the gap to the island. In desperation she peered from her lair, and the wolves sensed the motion. They went quiet.

Blood rushed to Liana's face. The raven's chilling song and the wolves' anticipatory breaths filled her with dread. It was quiet for the first time since the raven had brought the wolves to Liana. In desperation, she scurried out from beneath the log and stumbled to her feet. To her surprise, much of the fog had cleared and standing only a few hundred feet away was the pack. The wolves were in a loose semicircle on the ribbon of ice bordering the river. There were seven of them, and the largest, darkest wolf was in the middle. Their lingering stares pierced Liana's sensibilities.

"Go!" she screeched while waving her arms. "Go away! Go!"

Three of the wolves retreated a few feet back into the forest, but four others stood their ground next to the river. All four lowered their heads and stared intently. The largest met her gaze with his enormous grey eyes. The wolves appeared more alert and began to bray. Massive incisors were luminous in the muted light. Liana waved her knife and screamed again at the wolves. "Go! Go away!" she screeched. "I'll cut you!"

Defiantly, the largest wolf leisurely took a couple of steps toward the water. Liana gasped as she met his stare. He raised his head to the sky and the rest of the pack joined in a deafening salute. Their unison overwhelmed Liana's little voice, stomped it into the snow like a mouse. Dispirited, Liana stopped yelling and gasped at the intensity of the standoff.

The wolves held their ground, not intimidated by Liana's aggressive threats. Across the narrow band of water and ice they stood, all of similar proportions and colouring. The largest wolf had a grey muzzle and its left ear was broken and bent over half way to the tip. Their frosted muzzles opened on perfect ivory teeth, and their muscular, lofting haunches gave them the illusion of being as tall as caribou. Their breath hung in the air between them as they nuzzled each other and yelped. The raven sang with excitement.

The lead wolf raised his tail and suddenly the other wolves changed their tactics. The pack began charging up and down the river, searching for a crossing to the island. They divided: four went up river and two went down river. The wolves wove and darted among the dark trees and leafless willows and poplars, panting, barking, and yipping. But the lead wolf remained steady opposite Liana, staring with his expressive grey eyes.

Liana stood with her back against the log studying the commotion. The raven gurgled mysteriously. Liana bent down, reached through the snow, and snapped a fist-sized rock from the ice. She hid the rock under her sleeve so the raven couldn't see that she had it. The raven was on his perch on the root of the log and was less than twenty feet away. A moment later, with a swift, deliberate motion, she hurled the stone toward the bird. But the raven didn't even flinch, and the rock slipped into the snow short of the brazen creature with hardly a whisper. Liana dropped her shoulders and slumped at the hopelessness of her situation. The raven cawed louder at Liana's feeble attempt to silence it. Liana wanted to cover her ears and retreat under the log but didn't want the wolves to sense her fear or give the raven any satisfaction.

Glancing up the river she could see the four wolves converge on a small eddy. One of the smaller wolves stood tentatively at the edge of the ice and peered into the water. The other wolves yipped with excitement. The small wolf carefully stepped its two front paws off the ice shelf into the current. Its long legs fell into the water and its head went underwater unexpectedly. Its back legs followed; the wolf splashed into the river. In an instant its gaping maw shot out of the water and gasped for air. Its head emerged from the weak current and the hapless wolf stood in icy, chest-deep water. It struggled to climb on top of a large, smooth rock, but its front paws slipped and fell past its chest into the river with another splash. The weak current spun the helpless wolf, and it faced Liana and whimpered softly.

Liana knew that her best chance of defending herself against the wolves was aggression. She broke her quiet face-off with the lead wolf and ran toward the younger wolf stranded in the icy water. She clutched her knife and screamed, "C'mon! You want to come to my island?" The leader turned its head away, apparently disinterested in Liana's rant. Liana cut across the icy rocks toward the upstream end of the island. The young wolf raised its front paws onto the ice shelf and repeatedly tried to pull itself up and onto it, but with each effort plunged back into the river. The current was slowly dragging the creature downstream toward the island. The wolf bawled short, sharp cries of frustration at not being able to climb onto the ice. The other wolves watched in stillness, unable to help.

Liana yelled, "You're going to freeze! The raven will be eating your eyes by nightfall." She laughed at the wolf. The leader remained motionless, indifferent.

The young wolf swam close to the shore and in desperation lifted its two front paws onto the ice shelf. Its rear feet finally touched bottom and it tried weakly to pitch itself out of the river. It whimpered as it bounced its way downstream, pushed by the sluggish current. When the young wolf finally reached a shallower spot, it sprang instantly from the water and onto the ice. The immature wolf scampered clumsily and rolled on its back in the snow. Three wolves ran toward it and licked the young wolf's muzzle. The wolf regained its feet, shook violently, and dropped again onto its back, writhing in the snow in an effort to drain water from its fur. The wolf looked vulnerable and dejected to Liana. Wet and cold, it was much smaller than it had first appeared, even scrawny. It dropped onto its belly and licked the ice from between its toes in the same way Liana had seen huskies clean their feet after long sled trips. The defeated youngster paid Liana no attention even though it lay close to where Liana stood.

The other five wolves continued to search for a passage to the island and soon wore a path though the snow on the upstream and downstream sides of the shore. This deep trench spoke to their frenzied commitment to get to the island. The wet wolf ignored their efforts while the large wolf steadfastly watched Liana's movements. The bloodthirsty raven continued to sing its maniacal encouragement in boisterous throbs and shrieks.

When the wolves were unable to find a way to the island, they returned to the lead wolf. They grouped on both sides of him directly across from Liana and stared at her. Liana thought about a time when she and Henry had watched an older female wolf prep a small pack on the intricacies of hunting caribou. She had dug up a caribou leg she had cached earlier in the season. The less experienced wolves in the pack approached her from the front and she wagged her head from side to side as if to say "No." She then hit them with the leg as she ran past them to inform them of the risk of taking down large animals. The wolves rehearsed over and over in an elaborate instructional game. Henry told Liana that wolves commonly did this and it was often the smaller female wolves that were the best hunters. A lone wolf only took small animals like ground squirrels or rabbits, but in a pack they would take elk, caribou, bison, and moose—animals ten times their size. Many wolves were injured or killed hunting large game, mostly victims of kicks and goring. Henry said he thought the female was likely paired with the alpha male and was too valuable to risk hunting. Instead she had taken on the role of instructor, and patiently drilled the pack until they functioned as a single organism.

"These wolves are well schooled," thought Liana.

Liana held her ground on the beach and stared the largest wolf in the eyes. After a lengthy silence, he raised his head and started to howl. An enormous blare filled the valley and echoed off the canyon walls. When the wolf ended its call for a quick gasp of air, the rest of the pack joined the refrain and the intensity of their howls caused Liana to step backwards involuntarily. All seven wolves howled for as long as their lungs would allow. The echo made the howls sound like one breathless, constant salvo.

Liana stood in the cold and stared back at the pack. In her hand was her trusted knife. The wolves howled for hours and

Liana stood in the chill, facing the din. The light slowly began to fade as the sun tracked across the sky and behind the mountain ridges. Liana's ears ached with the wolves' breathless song, which never changed in tempo or intensity. Occasionally the raven would join the chorus with its own maniacal refrain. The raven's insistent calls, while not loud, were shrill enough to cut through the raucous symphony of wolf howls. Liana felt as though she were losing her mind. She stared at the raven. He stared back with a look of indignation and scorn.

As the night sky took over the indigo of evening, the northern lights once again appeared like a friend. Long sweeping streaks of emerald and pink whipped and sawed across the horizon somewhere between the stars and the northern forest. The howling seemed to intensify with the appearance of the brilliant display. It was almost as though the wolves had called the northern lights. Liana stood transfixed by the enormity of the sight. The howls ripped through her soul and the northern lights dizzied her with their quick swoops and pirouettes. It was the most intense moment Liana had ever experienced.

But eventually Liana grew exhausted from the barrage of howls and dizzying light display and was unable to withstand the brisk evening cold any longer. The wolves were not going to cross the river, at least not this night. They continued their chorus as she climbed under the log and slid into her icy lair. She held her hands over her ears, and in a silent convulsion, she cried. The howls were the worst sound she had ever heard and they resonated in the enormous valley for hours. The sound was unbearable and seemed to vibrate the very stones of the island. Liana cursed the raven as she covered her face and ears and sobbed in the dark. Time had stood still and she couldn't think of anything except the loud drone that pierced her very heart.

Liana cowered in her gloom through a haunted night. She kept her knees curled into her chest and protected herself as best she could from the dissonance. All her dreams were about wolves, especially the pack leader with the grey muzzle and intense eyes. She dreamed she had a gun and could shoot the raven first and then shoot the wolves one by one. She shot the large wolf last, right between its searching eyes.

Liana opened her eyes sometime mid-morning. The forest was hushed. The quiet startled her. She scrambled to a sitting position and peered into the brightness. Snow flurries filled the sky and the forest was still. Liana peered cautiously from beneath the log, squinting in the light that cleared the ridge. All she could see were footprints from the wolves' reconnoitering on the opposite bank.

"Were they able to cross the river somewhere else?" she wondered as she scrambled through the opening. A prickle of dread ran from head to toe as she stood beside the log and scanned both sides of the river. But she knew they were no more able to cross the river than she was. They had left because there was no way to reach her, and momentarily this thought gave her comfort. Then she realized that what protected her also prevented her escape. The raven watched silently from its perch on the root of the log. He turned his head and preened his wing feathers, unconcerned.

After so many days stranded on the island, Liana had no doubts: her days were numbered. Her weakness grew as the snow deepened. It concerned her that she no longer felt hungry, only cold. She slipped in and out of dreams all day and night as she lay curled in a ball trying to huddle any warmth that might remain. This morning she opened her eyes to another day of cold and quiet. She felt listless, bored, and alone. She peered above the stone wall in front of her sheltering log at the gloom. The snow had softened the silhouette of the distant forest. A thick drift also covered the ice shelf and the open river had narrowed to a ten-foot gap. The growth of the ice bridge from the shore to the island, once so crucial to her day and her very survival, now left her feeling indifferent. Thinking about the ice made her tired and impatient; she preferred to dream of her loving parents and Henry.

"How many days have passed since Henry died?" wondered Liana. She remembered him chopping wood the morning she left to go hunting. He stopped chopping only long enough to wish her good luck. It was awkward, since they both knew Henry's hunting days were behind him because his vision was so poor. She could hear the rhythmic crashing of the axe against the frozen wood as she climbed the trail to the plain.

Mornings were now the hardest part of the day. Shivering all night left Liana exhausted as she waited an eternity for the sun to clear the ridge. The dense presence of the cold settled into the valley and slowed everything. She felt coldest for the first hour after sunrise and was always disappointed by the weakness of the morning sun. The first few days on the island Liana had dreaded the dusk, since it brought the biting cold and oppressive dark, but now the futility of the new day bothered her most.

Liana tried to conserve as much of her core heat as she could. She lay on her side and curled her legs to her chest and tucked her hands under her arms. She wished she had some evergreen boughs to make a mattress, which would insulate her from the ground. The agony of spending so much time under the log and the pale chill of the winter was overwhelming. Aside from lying flat, the sleeping positions were basically the same and she only moved when her legs, neck, or back cramped and stabbed with pain. Liana assumed that there was no position she would find comfortable and accepted cramps as unavoidable. Even Liana's skin was dry and sore. Most of the time the sharpness of her discomfort awakened her from deep sleep and proved that she was still alive.

As winter deepened, the days grew only slightly less biting than the night. The mountains shielded the valley and allowed the night temperature to drop dramatically with each clear, still night. Without clouds to hold the sun's warmth, the thin night air plummeted into an arctic chill. "I'm falling apart," Liana said breathlessly from her cracked, faded lips. Suddenly, she remembered Henry telling her earwax could be spread on cracked lips.

As she soothed her lips, Liana cursed her father for bringing her to the North. After her mother's death, he roamed Paris for six months—a lost soul. And then one evening he burst into their apartment and said they were going to make a fortune in the Klondike Gold Rush. Liana was only ten at the time. But she was happy to see her father planning their escape to the goldfields. Anything was better than seeing her father as a broken man wandering the streets of Paris alone. They would both leave the heartbreak of her mother's untimely death behind.

The next day everything they owned was for sale on the street in front of their apartment. Liana sat next to her father on the curb and watched people haggle with him for the patchwork of their memories. The first thing to be sold was their mantle clock. It was heavy, and the brass-coloured clock sat inside a thick glass dome. The next thing sold was their kitchen table. Soon Liana's armoire and her father's books were gone as well. Their pots and pans, living room chairs, and hat stand walked away. An elderly woman offered a price to buy all her mother's clothing. Liana's father stared at her blankly and counter-offered; the woman passed him a crumpled handful of bills. Liana's heart sank as she watched the elderly woman stagger away under the awkward bail of clothing. During the next two days, Liana sat numbly beside her father and watched as everything she knew slowly disappeared.

In their empty apartment, Liana's father excitedly told her about how wealthy they were about to become. "There are nuggets just waiting to be picked up," he exclaimed. Liana knew about the Gold Rush. How could she not? Every magazine and newspaper had written about it for the past couple of years. The fact that her father seemed to think it had just started concerned her. When she asked him whether there would still be gold when they got there, he reassured her: "There's lots of gold. Don't worry."

Once everything was sold, they took a train at the Paris Metro bound for the coast. They arrived in Nantes, where they would spend a couple of days before boarding their ship. Liana's father found them simple accommodations near the harbour, and they carried their meager belongings to a spare hotel room. They ate bread and cheese quietly on their beds while listening to the ring of distant lighthouses and ship bells. Liana slept fitfully that night, unsettled to be leaving her beloved Paris.

In the morning they sat up in bed, their bags and clothes spread messily around the room, and ate the remaining stale baguette from the night before. They spoke softly about last minute travel details and the adventure they were about to begin. Liana dreaded traveling on the ship and being cooped up for almost two weeks, but her father reassured her that it would be okay.

In the afternoon they visited the Jardin des Plantes de Nantes, an ancient botanical garden. Even though it was October, the plants seemed to flourish. Her father told her of the legendarily cold December in the 1870s when most of the plants in the gardens had died. Nobody could remember a cold snap as severe, and the few magnolias and other plants that survived were so hardy that nothing could kill them. Liana marveled at the ordered gardens, the fountains, and the large man-made hill called the "artificial mountain."

Liana's father told her about Paul Marmy, the man who built the garden's spectacular palm house and orangery after the gardens had been neglected for decades. It was now twenty years later, and to Liana, the trees Marmy planted looked as mature as if they had always been there.

The visit to the gardens was a welcome relief from days of preparation and hurried packing. Liana felt it was the best day she had had with her father since her mother's death. She felt optimistic about the future because he was in such good spirits, and when he bought her a bag of toasted chestnuts from a street vendor Liana didn't think the day could get any better.

The next morning they boarded the SS *Kolata* and said goodbye to their old ways. They were bound for New York City and eventually a fresh start in the gold fields of the Yukon. The days on the ship passed slowly and Liana settled into a boring, repetitious routine. She rarely went above decks and kept mainly to their cramped stateroom. Her father, on the other hand, was never below decks except at night. Occasionally Liana ventured from their room to find him. He was always in the salon, listening to people talk about their travels. The main wave of gold seekers had left a couple of years before, so he wasn't able to find any kindred souls. Liana heard him ask one of the stewards about his brother. The steward looked weary of having the same conversation repeatedly with Liana's father, but politely explained that he hadn't heard from his brother since he had arrived in Dawson City. "He's probably filthy rich by now," said Liana's father proudly, "drinking the best champagnes France can spare!" The steward shrugged and busied himself clearing tables. Liana was starting to feel sorry for her father and his single-minded interest in the gold fields. Little else seemed to captivate him anymore.

Arriving in New York City was anticlimactic for Liana, the Statue of Liberty unimpressive. Her father pointed to it and said "That was France's gift to America," but Liana didn't really care. She was too tired and bored from the journey across the Atlantic. They were only in the city overnight and slept leaned against each other on a bench in the lobby of Grand Central Station. Their suitcases and bags stood at their feet.

In the morning they shared a chewy salted pretzel and boarded a train bound for San Francisco. The travel and disturbed sleep left Liana even more tired and overwhelmed, but as the train rattled and jerked out of Grand Central, her world started to feel expansive again. The confines of the ship were replaced by a coach seat with a large window to lean against and dream. The farmland and grey forests of the east gradually gave way to the silver prairie and mountains of the west.

In San Francisco they boarded a small, worn ship headed north. They pitched in the open oceans around northern California, Oregon, and Washington before entering the protected northerly waters of the Inside Passage off the coast of Canada. Vancouver Island and then the respite of the islands of the Alaska panhandle protected them from the chop of the North Pacific. As the turbulence subsided, Liana felt a greater peace traveling through the hundreds of miles of mist-shrouded fjords. Her father stared at the remote parade of mountains and bright glaciers in quiet contemplation. Liana snuggled into his arms and wondered how they would survive this foreign, fierce landscape.

After more than a week on the ship they approached their destination: Skagway, Alaska. Her father couldn't contain his glee. "We're here. We're at the start of the Klondike Trail," he all but exclaimed, but Liana was more reserved. She braced for the remaining part of the journey and was barely able to muster a smile for her father.

From the ship, Skagway seemed a cluster of shabby buildings at the base of impossibly steep mountains. It looked cold and raw and Liana felt hesitant to get off the ship. But as she walked down the gangplank, she squeezed her father's hand and was reassured by his commitment to their journey. As they collected their suitcases, Liana thought about how far she had come. They had crossed an ocean and traversed North America. They had plied the Pacific Northwest for more than a thousand miles before landing at the most peculiar place she had ever imagined. But she knew that the most challenging passage was still ahead. Staring at the seemingly impenetrable wall of mountains made her feel small and full of dread.

Skagway was a bustling boomtown. Broadway, the main street, was crowded with tent stores and false front buildings. Clusters of shaggy looking men crowded the streets and wooden boardwalks. The sounds of pianos and laughter emanated from seedy saloons that seemed to occupy every second building.

Liana clutched her father's arm as they struggled under the bulk of their bags and slowly walked from the wharf to the White Pass and Yukon Route Railway Station a few blocks away. Her father bought train tickets to Whitehorse, another grubby town they needed to pass through to reach Dawson City. Whitehorse was more than a hundred miles away, on the other side of the Coast Mountains and the Canadian border. Whitehorse was as far as the train went. From there it was either a paddlewheeler or horse-drawn sleigh to cross the remaining hundreds of miles north to mythical Dawson City. This late in the season, they would travel by sleigh.

Liana took a seat at the back of the depot. Her father piled their bags around her and then set out to get them something to eat and explore this shabby little town before their train arrived. As he walked out the door, he forgot to look back and

Liana felt small and inconsequential huddled amongst their meager possessions. She wiped a small peephole with her elbow through the condensation on the window and studied the busy little street. A team of what Liana thought were huskies was tethered to a sapling across the street. The dogs were hitched to a small wagon and seemed unconcerned with the bustle of the street. Liana had never seen anything like them before. She had heard of dogs being used to pull sleds but had never seen it with her own eyes. The sight was exotic and foreign to her.

Liana was curious about the street scene, but after several hours her father still hadn't returned and she became bored with the view. Liana thought about her father's wanderings in Paris and the way his absences had become both disappointing and familiar. She closed her eyes and napped, and when she awoke, the depot was bustling with activity. The train was about to arrive and porters prepared their carts and trolleys. When the train pulled in, scraggly men climbed down from the coaches and swung their canvas sacks and trunks onto their shoulders and disappeared into the crowded streets. She knew this was the train she and her father were supposed to take, but inherently understood her father wouldn't make it. Once again, Liana closed her eyes and rested under the wall of bags arranged at her seat. She wasn't disappointed to delay this leg of their journey.

In the morning her father woke her by holding a stale waffle under her nose. He stank of cigarettes and whisky but she was pleased to see him. Liana nibbled on the waffle and cleared the sleep from her eyes while he told her the stories he had heard in the saloon. They spent the rest of the morning with her father talking excitedly about the Klondike and how rich they were about to become. Liana was happy that her father was so excited and found the names of the people he was describing, like "Flapjack Pete" and "Poor House Jimmy," comical. And when the train pulled up to the depot they gladly climbed aboard and soon disappeared into the great northern forest with its impenetrable mountains and tumbling rivers.

After a day on the shaking narrow-gauge railway, they landed at Whitehorse, where they marveled at the enormous paddlewheeler ships that had been dragged from the river for the winter. Her father told her Dawson City was only a few hundred miles downriver, and with only a quick stop for the bathroom, they boarded a sleigh pulled by six large horses. They pulled heavy blankets made from wooly buffalo hides over themselves and braced for the cold. With a hearty crack of the whip, the coachmen signaled to the horses to begin the journey. The fresh snow was already rutted from horses and men, and the blades squeaked under the sleigh. Liana took a deep breath through clenched teeth. Her father's face beamed.

The path they followed was well travelled and they passed other sleighs every couple of hours. Every twenty miles or so was a simple log roadhouse where they would rest and eat deep bowls of greasy stew made from moose or whatever the proprietors had been able to shoot that fall. Most days they were able to visit three roadhouses and travel sixty miles. They changed horses at each roadhouse, and Liana enjoyed the pace of sleigh travel more than the ships and trains she had experienced on this trip. They arrived at each roadhouse exhausted but content with the progress north.

The coachman warned them that soon the quicksilver would register fifty below or even colder. The cold already had a volume Liana felt she could taste, and she was curious about the deep cold. But as the sleigh pulled them up the valley of the Yukon River toward Dawson City, Liana felt closer to her father than she had in months. The broad landscape with its distant mountains and vast river made her feel small and inconsequential.

Remembering her first impressions of the North and their journey to the Yukon comforted Liana. Since that first winter she had experienced minus-fifty temperatures before Christmas, and she knew it was possible this early in the winter for the mercury to drop that low. Her father enjoyed the phenomenon of spitting in the air and watching pea-sized frozen granules bounce off the ground. She knew she wouldn't last a night at that extreme. She had experienced the infamous mistral—the fierce winter wind that savaged Paris—but minus-fifty always felt surreal, like a brittle, somber dream. She never understood why her father was drawn to the North.

"Why did you choose this for us?" she sighed.

The looming trees were blasted with snow and frost. Branches creaked under the burden of the snow. Sometimes lingering sap froze in a trunk, and the sound rang out like a rifle shot. Most of the time, however, the forest was silent— dark and impassable as a high stone wall. During the day the trees along the bank were bathed in varying hues of blue. Light didn't penetrate past the front row of trees. Liana studied those that bordered the river and wondered what lay beyond.

She often imagined that she was someplace else, somewhere far from the bleak island. Her wandering mind whisked her back to France. Her parents hugged her; their bodies were soft, their skin smooth as silk. She could have stayed in their embraces forever. She walked to the patisserie for éclairs and croissants, which she dipped into deep bowls of hot chocolate. She imagined she could feel the warmth from the oven and smell the scent of butter and sugar. She saw her dog Pitou and gave him a foamy bath in a basin outside in the courtyard amid delicious sunshine and the scent of flowers. Sometimes she thought about her days in Dawson City with her father. She knew that she wasn't strong enough to think about the cabin and avoided drifting back upstream in her mind's eye.

Liana knew that the North would never be home again. She no longer found beauty in the great boreal forest, the high crags, or the cold lakes. She vowed that if she got off the island, she would leave the region forever. Bitter thoughts filled her until she had to leave her lair to get a drink of water. She climbed out of her enclosure in the lee of the big log, and the reality and disappointment of still being on the little island made her heart sink to unimaginable lows. In the relative comfort of her nest, island life was a bad dream.

"Why didn't I just drown?" she asked. "Just get it over with." The ritual of leaving the cavern for even a few minutes was now horribly difficult.

Her biggest challenge was motivating herself to check the slow progress of the ice. Most mornings the ice appeared to make little if any gain, and Liana's heart would become heavy and the day much colder. However, during the last week the ice had marched steadily and had almost entirely bridged the island to the mainland. The gap had become a narrow strip of river confined by a sharp, thick shelf of ice. The ice had thickened noticeably and Liana was feeling encouraged. The dark river wound a path between the island and the shore with a gap less than ten feet wide. Half this distance and Liana could have made an attempt to escape by jumping it.

This morning Liana drifted in and out of dreams especially easily. She worried momentarily if her end was near but then memories of warmth and food and family began to comfort her. She softly and slowly sang several verses from "On the Bridge of Avignon," a song she sang at home and in the schoolyard.

On the bridge of Avignon
Everyone is dancing
On the bridge of Avignon
Everyone is dancing in a circle.
The handsome men go like this.
And they go like that.

On the bridge of Avignon
The bridge of Avignon
Everyone is dancing
On the bridge of Avignon
Everyone is dancing in a circle.
The beautiful women go like this.
Then they go like that.
On the bridge of Avignon

On the bridge of Avignon
The bridge of Avignon
Everyone is dancing
On the bridge of Avignon
Everyone is dancing in a circle.
The gardeners go like this.
Then they go like that.

On the bridge of Avignon
The bridge of Avignon
Everyone is dancing
On the bridge of Avignon
Everyone is dancing in a circle.
The tailors go like this.
Then they go like that.

On the bridge of Avignon
The bridge of Avignon
Everyone is dancing
On the bridge of Avignon
Everyone is dancing in a circle.
The winegrower goes like this.
Then they go like that.

On the bridge of Avignon
The bridge of Avignon
Everyone is dancing
On the bridge of Avignon
Everyone is dancing in a circle.
The launderers go like this.
Then they go like that.

This simple folk song with the graceful movements of its accompanying dance reminded Liana of everything she had lost. Deep in her earliest memories, she heard her mother singing it at her bedside and she tried to sing along. When she used to stumble on the lyrics, she would ask her mother to sing more slowly. Her mother would smile patiently.

"Chantes plus lentement, Mama," she requested in a child's voice. She laughed as her mother reached the end of the song. "C'est bonne, Mama," she exclaimed with delight, clapping her hands softly. Liana was comforted by the softness of her mother's voice and smiled as she started to sing "On the Bridge of Avignon" again. Her voice trailed off as she squeezed under the log and lay on her back. Liana rested her head on her arm and rhythmically filled her chest with air. The confines of the lair were becoming familiar, and she knew that without the log, she would have been dead long ago.

The wolves had not returned for three days. Liana was still exhausted from their harassment and from the cold and the starvation and the loneliness and the million other things conspiring to drain her essence. She bristled at even the slightest whisper of wind and stayed holed up for all but the briefest escapes. The wolves' haunting cries and avid panting drilled into her brain so completely that the sounds felt like a part of her.

The creatures even appeared in her dreams. Her mother cautioned her to take good care of her pal Pitou so the Bois de Bologne wolves didn't eat him. The Gypsies cursed the wolves for stealing their fish. Liana's dream-self just shrugged knowingly and repeated with her mother, "Beware of the wolves. Beware of the wolves." In Paris, wolves seemed like creatures from a time gone by—like dinosaurs. "Did Mama mean wild dogs?" Liana wondered.

Liana softly hummed "On the Bridge of Avignon" and gradually awakened from her dream. Her swollen eyes blinked open, bloodshot and sore. The deceptive twilight of dreams was beginning to wear her down faster than the cold.

She wondered how the wolves could vanish so silently into the forest. "Only the raven knows where they are now. Perhaps they are still waiting" she thought.

The wolves had to be lurking somewhere. Their dark coats blended in so completely with the forest that she would never see them until it was too late. Liana began to hear their mournful howls again. The fierce, pulsating cries filled her cavern with an ever-rising pitch. Liana pulled her knees to her chest with her heart racing and held her hands over her ears defensively. But the howling was in her mind and could not be quelled.

"Am I still alive?" she wondered as she looked at her feet and arms and saw her breath hang in the air. "Of course I am," she reassured herself. "I'm just stuck. But why can't I feel the cold?" It was a vaguely worrisome thought. She had grown so accustomed to the depth of the pain from the cold that she had almost become immune to it. She was too exhausted and starved to feel the cold. Her ribs seemed to be emerging from her chest as the flesh around them shriveled. Her body was becoming a dry husk, an old pelt.

Liana thought about the largest wolf with its bent ear and unquestioned authority. As she remembered its thoughtful expression and questioning eyes, the howling became less intense and gradually faded.

"Perhaps that lead wolf will protect me from the other wolves," she thought. "Maybe it will show me the way out of the forest." She began to see the wolves differently. She saw them now not so much as a threat but as collaborators. For Liana it was easier to love than to hate.

The wolves energized Liana. She felt most alert when she thought of them, when she reacted to their threat. She dreamed of the wolves running across windswept lakes and through ragged mountain passes. They panted hard and their powerful legs propelled them tirelessly through crusty, windswept drifts. The pack bounded gracefully in organized, intuitive patterns like a school of fish changing direction in unison.

Sometimes Liana floated above them and encouraged them to keep up with her. They looked up at her and yipped.

Liana laughed in delight with their frustration. The moonlight cast long shadows throughout the forest and bathed everything in a silvery glow. They crossed an open meadow and traversed the dense forest together, the largest wolf in the front. She yelled an encouraging "Allons-y" when they yipped and howled at one another. The powerful wolves filled Liana with excitement and she effortlessly passed them, flying over the snow like a long-legged moose, and then was passed in turn.

Now breaking trail again, the wolves lead her over a small ridge, and she saw the lights of Dawson City in the distance. Liana ran to the lead wolf and pinched its bent ear affectionately as she passed. The wolf stared intently in the bright moonlight; his gaze seemed tender. Liana continued to run into the town then turned to see the wolves at the edge of the forest. They howled and Liana waved goodbye. She was finally home.

The sun twisted high in the sky when Liana first looked outside. It was bright for the first time in more than a week. There wasn't a cloud in the pale blue sky and the air was sharp as grit in Liana's throat. The snowstorm had left the forest under an even deeper layer of white, and the tree branches groaned and strained under the snow's weight. The drifts had already filled the wolves' tracks and the winding path up and down the shore was now hidden as well. There was no evidence that the pack had ever run along on the riverbank.

"Were they ever even here?" she wondered. The thought circled her mind like a buzzard, until suddenly it swooped away to target something on the ground: Perhaps the wolves were trying to help her escape the island. Liana propped herself up on one arm and considered this. The lead wolf's intelligent face with its grey muzzle filled her mind's eye. She could see its thoughtful expressions and compassionate eyes.

"Maybe he was trying to wake me up," Liana thought in the dank shadows of the log. "Maybe he hates the raven as well!" Liana felt encouraged as she lay back on the gravel, her heart racing. She imagined the leader's face stared intently at her. Its deep grey eyes studied her every motion patiently. The words "It's time to go" slipped from the wolf's mouth, though his muzzle did not move. Liana nodded in agreement. She again saw the wolves line the riverbank. She saw them run through thick forest and meadows, past frozen swamps and ponds and wooded mountain ridges. They wove and ducked and jumped over downed trees in a tapestry of movement. Liana heard their howls but no longer felt threatened by them. The wolves were not bloodthirsty; their cries encouraged her to fight the cold and escape the old log before it became her tomb. The endless cycle of running with the wolves swirled in her mind tirelessly, effortlessly. She ran with the wolves the rest of the night.

At first light Liana awakened to the miserable cry of the raven. She winced at its sharp cackles and croaks and stretched out in the darkened gloom of the log. She stared upward with her eyes wide open. It was the first sound the raven had made since the wolves vanished into the forest. The raven's songs were as mysterious as anything in the great forest. He sent forth a deep, guttural rebuke to Liana's will. The raven once more reminded Liana that it would wait to let cold and hunger do their work. The cold was inevitable, and the raven knew it wouldn't have to wait much longer. It held its solitary vigil, preening its shadowy feathers, waiting for Liana either to make a fatal mistake or simply succumb to starvation and exposure.

Liana felt alert and sat up. She placed her feet against the stone wall, braced her back to the log, and thrashed her feet. Her kicks had little strength behind them, but the wall collapsed one rock at a time. Liana kicked and kicked repeatedly. She didn't stop until almost all the rocks had tumbled into the snow and sun pierced the gloom. There was no turning back.

Liana squinted in the sunshine and inhaled the morning's calm, thin air. She looked upriver and could see that the ice had closed in on the hole at the bottom of the canyon. Soon the hole, like everything else, would be frozen into silence. Its maelstrom would be quieted to a muffled gurgle until spring, when the roaring tiger would be unleashed once again. Liana felt encouraged by its diminished threat.

"How long have I been here?" she wondered. She should have kept a record with notches in the log. It was too late now. Time had become an abstract thought that she rarely considered.

The raven screamed again and Liana instantly lost her calm. She felt rage course through her veins. Her ears burned with his insistent laugh. Her lips cracked and her body became more clumsy and uncoordinated. She climbed out from under the log and struggled to her feet. Furious, and without looking down, she stumbled on the remnants of the stone pony wall. Her body was stiff from being underground, but the morning sky invigorated her. Liana took a deep breath and waited for her eyes to adjust to the brilliant sunlight. She covered them until she could view the sparkling island without wincing.

She turned and trudged though the calf-deep snow. The drifts made it much more difficult to reach the river. As she had suspected, the ice shelf had not only almost closed the gap, but had also thickened and no longer cracked under her weight. Liana marveled at the sight of the almost continuous ice shelf between the island and the forest.

She bent down at the edge of the ice and reached her hand into the clear river; the current pulled weakly around her open hand. The water purled around her fingers and she smiled broadly. Liana studied the twinkling water moving between her fingers. She cupped a slurp of water and let it trickle over her chapped lips and thought about the Gypsy fish tickler. She felt the stab of cold water drop into her empty stomach. Winter had settled into her soul. Liana didn't fight the cold any longer; it was too complete and absolute on the little island. Cold was just a fact of life, like breathing. On this day, cold didn't even seem to exist.

Liana stood, shook water drops from her hands, and wiped her mouth on her sleeve. She took a good look at the river and the progress the ice had made and thought wistfully about her mother's hot chocolate. When Liana was a little girl, she would sit eagerly on a red wooden chair in their small kitchenette. Her mother stirred a pot with her back to Liana, humming a familiar song, and then dropped a large piece of chocolate into the saucier with a great splash. The sound made them both laugh. Young Liana eagerly waited for the frothy mixture but was just happy to be in the kitchen with her mom.

Liana inhaled the rich warmth of chocolate easing slowly into milk. The scent was tinged with something new—something she could not identify in the small kitchenette. As she considered the source, Liana was suddenly brought back to the island. "Fire!" a man's voice called through the stillness. "Fire!" echoed through the forest. Liana scanned the beach for the source of the alarm. She looked on both sides of the river. Again the call came, only softer. "Fire!" Liana hung on this word and scoured the beach. The muted hush of the wind drifted through the trees and filled her heart. Liana smiled gently at the familiarity of the games the forest played. She didn't trust the sounds any longer and didn't yell a response.

Liana studied the forest. The willow trees along the edge of the river bent under the heft of the snow and many branches were pinned to the ground. The coarse bark of the pine and spruce trees were dusted in snow and frost. Snow had been blasted into every crevice in the forest and it looked as finely detailed as marble sculpture, even from a distance. There was little colour in the forest aside from the dark evergreens. Liana squinted at the unfolding landscape. "It's time," she thought.

Liana turned again to the log and examined the stones freshly scattered around it. The hollow in the gravel and sand suddenly looked like a grave. Liana turned away from the log and stumbled through the snow, searching for the narrowest part of the gap in the ice. Near the bottom end of the island, the gap appeared narrowest. "It must be less than five feet," she thought. "Can I jump that?" Her legs were already tired from walking through the snow. "How can I walk anywhere if I am so weak?" she thought glumly. And then she felt the presence of the wolves and thought about them effortlessly cruising the vast forest. Just then, the raven broke its silence and brayed at Liana menacingly. Liana glared at the raven, perched twenty feet from her on the uppermost root of the log. The sun was behind him and Liana had to hold a cupped hand over her eyebrows in order to see the silhouette of the black bird. The raven called a single rebuke and Liana smiled knowingly at the bird.

Liana closed her eyes momentarily and cleared her mind. With a deep breath she drew her knife from the leather sheath on her waist. She unfolded her father's Laguiole and held the thin handle securely in her palm. The blade glinted in the sunlight and seemed to animate the raven, which craned its neck to see what Liana was doing. With her other hand she lifted her jacket and pulled up her shirts and turned her good hip toward the daylight. Her skin felt the draught and her awareness piqued with anticipation. She took a deep breath and dug her heels into the frozen sand of the beach. In a quick motion she sliced a slit in her skin. She looked numbly at the cut and the dark blood that filled the wound. She then placed the knife a short distance away from the first incision and pressed on the blade as she took a second slice. This time she didn't hesitate and the two parallel cuts separated a chunk of flesh. Her hand carefully removed this bit of her self. Strangely, the wound didn't hurt and Liana's eyes didn't well with tears. She held a woolen sock against her hip and placed the bait on the log and looked into the distance beyond the short gap in the river and the forest that stretched up the mountain ridges and out of sight.

Liana leaned her hip against the log with the sock bunched against it. This freed both her hands and she took the bloody bait and threaded it carefully onto the fishhook. She took a deep breath and squinted in the sun as she stood up. She looked at the attentive raven that was perched high above the log. She took a couple of slow steps through the fresh snow, trying not to scare it away or bleed excessively. The bird was still fifteen feet above her, with a vantage point of the entire island. The raven looked surprised by Liana's approach but didn't fly away. It felt unthreatened on its perch, where it bore witness to Liana's slow decline. It knew that her eyes would soon be its feast. This dance had gone on long enough for both of them.

Liana's gaze met the raven's and in an uncomfortable moment Liana felt remorse for the soulless bird. The raven shifted its weight from foot to foot and shook its head. Liana pulled her arm back and lobbed the baited hook toward it. The bait landed in a tempting, bloody spurt on the top of the log. The raven tilted its head to one side with curiosity. Instinctively, it jumped from the root and drifted with its wings outstretched toward the bait. The raven landed about fifteen feet away from Liana on the top of the log. It stood over the flesh and stabbed its beak at the bait. The raven lifted its head and in single gulp, swallowed Liana's flesh and the small metal hook. The sharp barb dropped into the raven's throat and snagged the soft tissue of its esophagus. Liana gasped as she saw the surprise in the raven's fearsome, shadowy eyes.

At that instant the raven realized its folly and its eyes met Liana's. With a gagging, painful choke, the bird cawed a panicked shriek that ripped through the forest's stillness. The raven lunged awkwardly into the sky. It unfolded its wings and took one snapping flap before reaching the end of the line. Using all her strength, Liana held the taut line fast and watched as the raven wheeled and spun before crashing into the snow with a soft hush. Liana deftly pounced on the raven and grabbed a wing with both her hands; the raven screeched in terror. It tried to stand up but Liana lifted her foot and crushed an outstretched wing under her boot. The raven screeched in agony and tried to scramble toward the river. But Liana still had a hold of the broken wing and the fishing line, which tugged at the raven's throat. She pulled the bird onto its back. The frantic raven pecked at her hand with its sharp beak, its dark eyes engorged with terror, but Liana didn't flinch. The frightened raven saw the sole of her boot rush toward its head. Mercifully, the pop of the raven's skull under Liana's boot ended the flurry. One of the raven's legs twitched momentarily before its whole body and the forest were still.

Breathing hard from her efforts, Liana gaped at the raven's deformed shape in the snow. A few blue-black feathers were scattered around her, the paths and marks telling the story of the fight and ultimate demise of the bird. Blood dotted the bright snow, though to whom it belonged, Liana could not say.

Liana held her hand against the wound on her hip to staunch the blood. She looked into the dark forest, her breath heavy. She reached down and picked up the raven by its scaly feet and dragged it back to the log. She threaded the maze of scattered rocks and sat in her lair. As calm returned, she pulled the raven's deformed body toward her. She studied the figure and marveled at its immense size. Its wingspan was easily three feet wide and it weighed at least a few pounds. Liana fanned its shining wing feathers in her hands. Blue-black and coarse, the corpse was limp, warm, and pliable. Its surprised eyes were wide open. She wanted to open her jacket and hug the warmth to her chest.

Liana felt optimism, a sensation she hadn't experienced since washing onto the little island. She laughed as she let the raven's wings flop into the snow. Optimism turned to triumph: "You didn't get my eyes after all!" she gloated. Her thoughts leapt to the wolves. She thought about the pack leader's soft, intelligent eyes and the way he would probably find the irony in the raven's fate. Liana grinned at her vanquished foe and felt a sense of peace. Her tormentor was gone.

Liana drew her knife across the raven's abdomen and opened the bird wide. She then cracked the chest into two pieces with all her strength. Liana felt the wet warmth of the raven's insides. She reached into the raven's abdomen and grabbed its intestines and guts—the heat startled her. Her fingers, cold for so long, savoured the warmth, and she grew excited by the sensation. With a shaking hand Liana pulled at the entrails and cut bite-sized pieces with her father's knife. She eagerly lifted the first piece to her mouth. She sucked the meat off the knife and warmth trickled down her throat and the salty blood stung her parched lips. Her heart raced with anticipation. She quickly dropped another morsel into her mouth and gulped it down. The unctuous taste of blood filled her mouth and Liana felt energy surge within her fragile body. In a frenzy she devoured the bird, cracking the bones with her teeth and fingers. She sucked marrow, juices, and bitter essence from the raven until only a dry husk of feathers and bones remained. Liana finally sat back, her fingers and face covered in runny blood and black feathers. Her stomach was distended and full for the first time in weeks. It seemed to glow behind her ribs.

Liana reclined against the log and studied the remains of the raven. Her side stung and she staunched the cut on her hip with her sock. The sun was high in the sky and Liana shielded her eyes with her hand and looked at the gap separating the island from the shore. "How far can I jump?" she thought. The gap seemed insignificant for the first time.

She slowly stood up and stared at the distant forest. Liana touched the silvery log momentarily and felt its smooth, barkless trunk. It had been a friend for which she was thankful. Then, pushing herself away from the log, she charged through the deep snow toward the river. She bounded through the powdery snow with an unfamiliar lightness and vigor. When she reached the edge of the ice, she launched herself off the ground and hurtled through the air and into the void.

To Liana, the island looked small and lonely from the distance of the forest. The grey log made her shudder. Black feathers and trampled snow were all that were left to tell the story of her survival in that fearsome place. For several minutes she stood and stared at the starkness she had endured. A single wolf call filled the emptiness with its plaintive call.

She glanced upstream to the distant canyon with its imposing walls. She then turned downstream and started to walk toward town. She felt weak but invigorated to be off the island and to have her belly full. Rivulets of blood seeped down her right side from the cut. She rhythmically lifted her knees and plunge-stepped through the thigh-deep snow. Liana was grateful to be moving.

"We did it," she told herself. "Henry helped me. Anything is possible."

Liana stayed on the river. The vegetation on the shore was thick and the progress would be slow and arduous. It was still early and she was optimistic that she would find shelter around each corner. She tried to move quickly but was weak and knew she was not making good time. But she persevered through the snow. Her feet grew wet and cold from the melting snow in her boots. She knew she had to get to somewhere warm before nightfall, as the chill factor would be extreme without the shelter of the log. In the open and exposed it was likely she still would perish. This thought carried her down the trail. "I can get to town," she told herself. "I can do this."

The midday sun was a relief. While the temperature was still below freezing the warmth of the sun gave Liana renewed hope. She squinted in the glare off the snow and ice and determinedly trudged down the frozen river.

Liana did not pass any berry bushes or other edible plants with which she was familiar. Besides, it would have been impossible to stop to eat, as the dark would be upon her in less than five hours. She did the math in her head and felt she might be able to travel ten miles before nightfall. She thought it was possible that someone lived on the river in the next ten miles. There were trappers spread throughout this country.

Each footstep brought her closer to town but she tired quickly. She was exhausted from her time on the island. The effort of walking through thigh-deep snow brought fatigue beyond any tiredness she had ever felt. Her feet felt like ten-pound weights were attached to them. But she felt invigorated to finally have escaped the island and her tomb under the log. She licked a bit of salty blood from a finger.

Bend after bend the river meandered. "Why not here?" she thought with each river bend she crossed. Liana followed its serpentine course to her uncertain future until late in the afternoon. As the light was fading, Liana noticed a blaze on a large spruce tree. The blaze was facing the river as a marker for someone traveling upstream.

"Perhaps this is a good fishing spot?" she considered.

"More likely," thought Liana, "this could be a landing for a cabin." Trying not to get her hopes too high, Liana circled the blazed spruce and noticed that someone had cleared away the under brush to form a 15-foot clearing. To Liana is seemed like a good spot to land a freighter canoe.

"You could tie up to the spruce tree and unload your supplies here," she said excitedly. Liana searched for a path and saw what could be a faint trail leading through the thick forest and up the hill.

"It may be nothing," thought Liana, "but I've got to check; nightfall will be in an hour."

In an instant Liana made a decision and began to break a trail up the hill. The path was narrow and winding. Snow-laden willow trees draped over the trail and as Liana pushed past them snow fell on her. She put her hands in front of her face and pushed through the willows fiercely. Eagerly she looked ahead to see what was along the trail and where it would lead.

As she crested the hill she spotted the ridgeline of a building. She stepped a little closer and saw a small log cabin nestled in a grove of aspen trees. The roof held a couple of feet of snow. It had a rough-hewn door and a small window next to it. At least a cord of wood sat on the porch beside the door. There was no path to the door, no smoke issuing from the chimney; the cabin seemed deserted. Elated, Liana ran to the door and pushed it open with her shoulder. Inside the dim interior sat a cot and a cast iron wood stove. In the corner was a table holding a box of tinned food. "It's a dream!" said Liana, closing the door.

The cabin's interior was as cold as it was outside. Liana twisted the damper control on the wood stove and then with a sharp screech swung open the heavy door to its wood box. Inside sat some newspaper with kindling on top of it. As was tradition in the North this was a "single match fire"—waiting to succor the cold traveler. Liana took a match from a box on the table and struck it on the sandpaper on the side of the box.

A rich orange flame burst into her fingers and she squinted in the smudge of sulfur fumes. She delicately placed the match on the newspaper. The fire ran along the edge of the news paper momentarily and then engulfed the entire sheet. Within seconds the kindling had also caught fire and a low roar reverberated in the stovepipe. Tired beyond belief, Liana stumbled backwards and fell on her backside. She stared in disbelief at the fire through the open door of the woodstove. Soon she would be warm.

After watching the dappled licks of flames for a few minutes, Liana carefully pushed herself to her feet and stumbled stiffly toward the table. It was a cornucopia, a feast just waiting for her arrival. She reached for the closest tin and the can opener that was next to it. Her hands were shaking but she was able to puncture the tin with the small implement and slowly pierce the tin open. Careful not to cut herself on the jagged lid, she tipped the can on its end and held its lip to her mouth. But like everything else the food inside the tin was frozen solid. Disappointed but aware of this reality Liana turned and placed the tin on top of the stove. She then opened a few other tins with the can opener and placed them one by one on top of the stove. By this time the stove was starting to radiate warmth. Liana sat in front of the roaring blaze straddling her legs on both sides of the stove. The room still felt frigid as a tomb and the sides of the wood stove were not yet warm, but it felt glorious. Liana kept the door to the stove ajar and let the heat play on her palms. The radiating pulses of warmth made her feel drowsy. As the day quickly darkened to night Liana marveled at what this day had brought. The island was behind her and the taunting of the raven had ceased forever.

Liana stepped outside the cabin to get more wood and looked down the hill at the icy river. The river shone in the last of the daylight. She gazed upstream and saw the river disappear into hills and distant mountains. "Somewhere up there was Henry's cabin," she exhaled softly. Liana picked up a couple of split logs from the woodpile and carried them into the cabin. She made a few more trips and laid the logs next to the stove so they would be as dry as possible. She filled a pot with snow and slid it on top of the stove to melt. She then stuffed three logs into the stove and sat on the edge of the cot. She leaned over and removed her sodden leather boots and wet woolen socks. Her feet were pale and wrinkled, but she had escaped frostbite. She lifted her shirt and examined both hips—one was almost healed into an angry purple welt. A thin open wound and a trickle of blood showed on the other side. Liana pulled herself on to the cot and climbed under the heavy woolen blankets. She stayed fully dressed, as the air in the cabin was still bitingly cold. She stretched on her back and her eyes soon slid shut.

When Liana awoke the cabin was pitch black and cozy. She could hear a loud wolf call and it reminded her of what she had escaped. Her head ached and her hip throbbed. Reluctantly she sat up in a fog of alertness and felt the dense throb of her temples. She stepped onto the cold floor and carefully tottered to the wood stove. With a screech she cranked the door open. Only a few embers remained in the wood box and Liana quickly resurrected the fire by adding a few pieces of kindling, which smoked at first. Soon bright licks of flame ran along their length. She placed a couple of smaller logs on top of the kindling and waited at the open door for them to catch fire. The fire mesmerized Liana and she stared at it bewildered. She had been cold for so long that it seemed impossible to be in a cabin with food and warmth.

She reached onto the woodstove and took the pot of lukewarm water and took several massive gulps. The warm water trickled into her chest and her throat felt raw and sore. Liana then reached for the first opened tin on top of the stove and slopped some of the contents into her mouth with a broad spoon. The excruciatingly sweet perfume of cherries filled her head and made her wince. The sweetness was foreign and almost unpleasant. She swallowed unhurriedly and then filled her mouth with a second sloppy gulp. The soft texture and fragrant intensity of the fruit made her heart race. It was a firecracker of sensation. Liana took more gulps and soon the tin was empty and thick warm syrup dripped down her chin.

The other tins beckoned, but Liana remembered Henry telling her about the danger of eating too much at once after a long time without food; like so many other things, he had known hunger. Liana made the decision to wait to eat more food. Her stomach groaned in its effort to digest the cherries. She didn't want to get sick and knew that it would take a long time to regain her strength.

Liana strained to remember a story Henry had told her: An old man living in Alaska had lost all of his friends and family, and he felt sad to think that he was left alone. While this man was traveling along the woods, it occurred to him to go to the bears and let the bears kill him. But when he saw a bear he became frightened and told the bear "I want to invite you and the other bears to a feast." He then went home to prepare for the feast. Once all the food was laid out, he took off his shirt and painted himself with stripes of red across his arms, a stripe over his heart, and another stripe across his chest.

The bears arrived the next morning and the man let them into his home. First he served them large trays of cranberries preserved in grease. The large bear seemed to say something to his companions, and as soon as he began to eat the rest started. They watched him and did whatever he did. The man followed that up with other kinds of food, and after they were through, the large bear seemed to talk to him for a very long time. When the large bear finished, he started out, and the rest of the bears followed. As they went out, each in turn licked the paint from the man's arm and chest. The old man felt as though they were licking his sorrow away.

The day after all this happened the smallest bear came back in human form and spoke to the old man. He had been a human being who was captured and adopted by the bears. This bear-man asked the old man if he had understood their chief, and the man said he did not.

"He was telling you," the bear-man replied, "that he is in the same condition as you. He, too, is old and has lost all of his friends. He told you to think of him when you are mourning for your lost ones."

The cabin's interior flickered in the glowing radiance of the wood stove's little glass window. On the cot, Liana propped herself on one arm still in disbelief at her good fortune. She ran her hand over her ribs and marveled at how thin she was. She felt her flat stomach and almost absent breasts. And once again Liana drifted to sleep.

When she awoke she was startled to not be in the confines of the log on the island. It was morning and the sun shone through the one tiny window beside the door. The cabin felt warm and inviting and Liana was covered in a layer of sweat.

"Being warm is going to take some getting use to," she thought.

She pushed the coarse blankets to the side of the bed and kicked them away with her feet and stood carefully. The wooden floor was cold to her bare feet and she leaned toward the half dozen logs next to the stove. She lifted the heated pot of water to her lips and took a small slurp. She let its warmth radiate though her torso and immediately she felt like she was going to be sick. She stepped backwards and dropped onto the bed. Liana rested her head between her legs, the room lightly spinning.

"It doesn't take much these days," she thought wryly.

After a few minutes Liana stood carefully and padded toward the table, resting her hand on the table top for stability. She looked at the tins of food with soft focus and picked up the partially eaten tin from earlier. Without reading the label of the tin she dipped a spoon into congealed gravy and lifted out pieces of carrot and potato. She hesitated momentarily before spooning these morsels past her swollen, reddened gums. The oily richness of the gravy filled her mouth with an almost unbearable intensity and in a few enormous gulps the entire can was finished. Liana examined the label and the picture of the stew before placing the empty back on the table.

Liana stuffed another few logs into the woodstove and staggered back to the cot and stretched out. Under the log she always curled into a ball; being able to stretch her body filled her with a tingling sensation. In another moment she was asleep once again.

It was midday when she awoke. The cabin was much warmer and Liana's head ached. She lay on the cot for several minutes taking in her new surroundings. It was a small cabin, like most trappers' cabins. Whoever owned it had taken care to chink the logs with moss and scraps of wood. This chinking kept the cabin warm and somewhat draft free. The cabin was dark in even the brightness of the day. On the wall by the door was a calendar with "1899" written across the top. "A year old," thought Liana. Once again she heard the shrill tremolo of the wolf.

Liana carefully climbed out of bed and once again fed kindling to the dying embers. The fire quickly leapt to life and before long a roar raged in the wood box. Liana slid her boots on her feet without socks. Her boots were wet and cold to the touch. She was thirsty again. Next to the door was an enamel bucket; she picked it up and stepped outside. The air felt cold compared to the inside of the cabin and she squinted in the brightness of the afternoon. Liana dipped the bucket into a snowdrift. She then walked back into the cabin and placed the bucket on the stove where it hissed loudly.

Liana walked over to the pile of tins and examined their labels. Mostly they were just canned cherries and stew. She took a can of stew and worked the can opener to reveal its moist interior. She placed the can on top of the wood stove next to the bucket and climbed back into bed. Liana laid on her back because both sides were too sore and she had never liked lying on her stomach. Liana looked at the stovepipe and its exit through the roof of the cabin. Her head ached, as did everything else. Her mouth was dry and her stomach groaned in confusion.

After about half an hour Liana got out of bed and got a tin cup from the table. She poured water from the bucket into the cup and slowly sipped it. Her lips stung and she remembered that the salt from the stew must still be on her lips. She licked her lips clean and reached for another tin of warmed stew. She dipped her spoon into the stew and ate a little more slowly. The stew felt strange warmed and she could feel it drop down her throat and dissipate its warmth to her fragile body.

When she was finished eating Liana sat and looked at the fire. She thought about Henry.

"He would have loved this cabin," she thought. She had not allowed herself to dwell on Henry's death because she feared falling apart. But now warm and fed and alone it was all she could think about. She sat on the edge of the bed and for the first time she allowed herself to weep out her mourning. Her body convulsed with sobs and deep gasps. Henry was gone and she felt an emptiness that frightened her. Tears crossed her swollen cheeks and her body shook. Liana fell back onto the cot.

For the next week she cried and ate, cried and slept, cried and fed the fire. When she could cry no more she got out of the bed stronger than she had been in weeks.

Liana wanted to leave the cabin as strong and healthy as possible. She melted snow in both buckets and undressed to have a bath. She found a sliver of soap and made a rich lather on a faded rag. First she washed her hands and face, the soap hardly foaming in the accumulated grime. The soap smell stung the tip of her nose and made her sneeze. Cautiously she dipped her head into the bucket and braced herself breathlessly and washed her hair. It required several buckets of water heated over the course of an afternoon for her to finally begin to feel clean. Liana even washed her shirts, socks, and underwear but didn't attempt to clean her jacket or pants. She liked feeling clean and it felt good to be busy. Her hips hadn't throbbed in days.

One clear morning she awoke, dressed, and prepared to walk to town. She had been at the cabin for almost a month and was starting to run out of food. She adjusted the knife on her belt. It was now mid-winter and the daytime temperatures weren't much warmer than the nights. The snow was deeper and the air bitingly cold. But she was strong enough to survive the walk.

Liana didn't re-stoke the fire but simply left it to slowly die out. She put on her jacket and wrapped a blanket over her shoulders like a shawl. She pulled her hat over her brow, shut the cabin door firmly, and stepped off the porch into the bright morning.

Liana walked down the trail to the river. She felt strong and the crunch of dry snow under her feet filled her with optimism. Snow had covered the tracks she had made when she first arrived and she relied on the blaze to lead her back to the river. She stumbled through the deep snow to the bottom of the hill and then walked onto the river, now fully frozen. She plunge-stepped through the powdery snow. It was slow going but faster than bushwhacking through the forest. Liana was invigorated to be moving again.

Liana moved quickly and rarely stopped to catch her breath or take a mouthful of snow. The snow felt like hard candy and slowly dissolved in her mouth and quenched her thirst. By dusk she had made good progress. "Maybe ten miles, probably more," mused Liana. But the dark made it impossible to avoid stumbling. It was too dark to walk forward and she didn't want to build a shelter so she waited an hour. Once the moon cleared the treetops, the frozen river became an illuminated path. The snow glistened in the pale yellow light and Liana was able to make good progress walking in the silvery moonlight. In the far distance she could see the lights of the town light up the mountainside. It would take all night but she would get there.

I t was dawn when Liana saw the distant silhouette of the buildings and tents of Dawson City. After a day and a night of walking, she reached the outskirts of the grim little town. She felt invigorated to have finally reached her goal. While Liana trudged through the snow, she thought about something Henry had said many times: "Fear makes the bear look bigger." She felt enormous gratitude to him now for protecting her from Cody. She wondered how she would react when she finally met him. She fingered the outline of her knife: cold comfort.

From the river the town looked small and randomly built. Faded cabins, shacks, and hotels were arrayed in a cluster through the milky fog. Large spruce mooring posts for paddlewheelers bordered the bank in front of her. The boats were floating hotels that carried in most of the town's supplies. They were lifelines to the outside world when the river was running. Liana had seen paddlewheelers lined three deep in a frantic effort to unload supplies under the midnight sun of summer. Crews knew that the more trips they made, the more money they would earn and pushed themselves to unload as quickly as possible. When the boats made the return trip upriver to Whitehorse or down to St. Michaels, they were always almost empty. Often the only passengers were the broken and destitute, though at the end of the season successful prospectors with satchels and canning jars filled with gold would bow the gangplanks of the vessels to spend the winter in the cities of the west. As she wallowed through the soft snow and tangled willows of the steep bank and plunge-stepped past the mooring posts and onto the packed snow of the wagon road, Liana thought of traveling home to France and never returning to the North again. The wolf's piercing call reminded her of her escape from the wilderness.

During the summer, the streets of Dawson City were either unbearably dusty and dirty or so muddy they would bog down horse-drawn wagons. However, most of the year, its icy rutted streets were easier to travel. She passed a group of six ravens sitting on a fence. She looked away and felt her heart race. Fortunately they did not pay her any notice and she was grateful.

The town was quiet, with barely a person in sight. Liana turned onto Broadway and walked past stores, saloons, restaurants, and hotels. The town was only a few years old but already it seemed beaten up and worn out. Acrid wood smoke stuck in the back of her throat and burned her eyes.

"Henry never liked this town," she thought. She remembered him saying that even before the Gold Rush, his people would trade there and it was buggy because of the swamps.

"But it was good for moose," he said, laughing. It was a hodgepodge of tents, privies, and false front buildings that Liana always found distasteful and coarse.

When gold was discovered in Nome, Alaska, Dawson City emptied overnight. The miners raced down the Yukon River for the frozen beaches of Nome in rough built scows and rafts. In its heyday, more than thirty-thousand lost souls called Dawson City home. But now it was different; Liana could feel the desperation in its streets without going into a single building. Large commercial dredges had replaced the pick axes, gold pans, and rocker boxes of the early arrivals. The handful of Stampeders who remained worked on these noisy mechanical monsters, trapped by the monotony of labouring for large companies. Cody's days, like almost everybody's in Dawson City, were numbered.

As she had done many times, Liana detoured on the second street she came to. She turned away from the river and walked up a long hill to the base of the ridge known as the "Dome." The cabin she had lived in with her father was covered in deep snow and smoke roared from its chimney. Liana did not know who lived there now and did not care to knock on the door to find out. She gently opened the gate to the cabin and walked to the backyard. A thick stand of poplar trees crowded the back corner of the lot. Liana's father always told her that any miner worth his salt hid his poke outside. Anybody could find it inside—but outside, if you were careful, you were safe.

"Never put your poke in the bank," he cautioned. "Not only will the government steal it through taxes, but also it only takes one crooked bank manager to leave you with nothing." He never offered much advice to Liana, but like most prospectors, he had strong opinions when it came to gold.

Liana had seen her father shimmy up these trees a couple of times at night when he thought she was asleep. Liana placed her hands around the narrow trunk of the first tree and slowly and deliberately worked her way up. Soon she was fifteen feet off the ground and was able to reach the first branch. She pulled herself up and looked into its crook but didn't see anything. She carefully raised her hand and brushed away the snow, dipping her hand into the space. The poke wasn't there, though she was confident it was somewhere in the grove. Liana pulled her feet higher up the trunk and cradled them in the crook. She stepped the gap to the next tree, two feet away, and searched again. After she had searched four trees this way, she spotted it: a tobacco tin partially covered by snow. Liana opened her knife with one hand and cut the rawhide lace that secured the tin to the tree. She tucked the tin in her pocket and shimmied to the ground, making a whumping sound when she landed. On the ground she opened the tin and saw a cluster of gold nuggets.

"Thanks, Papa," she said quietly. Then she glided purposely out to the street without making a sound.

The town was starting to stir and wagons creaked and cracked as their wheels shuddered on the thin ice of the rutted, frozen streets. Smoke from every building and tent masked the morning's sunshine. Small packs of mangy huskies and malamutes were sprawled on the wooden boardwalk wherever the sunlight hit. A distant church bell rang to say it was Sunday, the only day of rest in the frontier town. It was the day when miners would hike in from their claims to eat and drink and share some human companionship.

Liana strode straight to the Tivoli Hotel at the far end of Broadway. It was a white building with "Tivoli" painted across its facade in large block letters. Through the front windows, Liana could see several tables of men scattered around the foyer. She walked up the icy steps, opened the door, and entered the moist, warm gloom as if she did so every day. The dozen or so men scattered around the room didn't pay her any notice and she took a seat near a window. Liana hung her jacket on the back of her chair. A waitress immediately approached her but before she got to the table, Liana said, "I'll have a cup of coffee and a glass of water, please." She ordered while gazing at the floor. The waitress spun to get the coffee. The men talked in hushed tones.

Liana looked out the window at the frozen town. From a couple blocks away she spotted Cody. He always walked briskly. Sunday morning was no different than any other. For a hustler, every day was a work day.

Cody was likely tired, Liana thought. Even though the mounted police always shut down the town at midnight on Saturdays, in Dawson City there was always an after hours game of chance or entertainer to chaperone. She knew she would be safe if she met him in a public place like a restaurant. She also knew that if she went into his hotel, she would never come out.

The last time she had seen him was in the Monte Carlo Saloon with her father. Cody had spent the night gambling and had bet $5,000 on a single hand of stud poker. He never trusted Faro, with its ancient origins. But stud poker, with its simple rules and opportunities for bluffing, suited him well. According to the story they were told by one of Cody's men, he held three of a kind but was beat by a full house. Cody bellowed at the crowd, "I must be the unluckiest sucker ever to set foot in the gold fields!" This brought much laughter and became the buzz of the town, repeated like a headline from the latest newspaper. That morning Cody shook hands with Liana's father and agreed to grubstake his claim. Her father was reluctant to be in business with Cody but pleased to have an investor all the same. Cody barely noticed Liana, except to tip the brim of his hat in her direction when they left.

When Cody stomped into the Tivoli, the other diners sat up and took notice. His five-foot-five frame demanded attention. His arms were thick and his barrel chest was as pronounced as a great ape's. Cody's movements were exaggerated, almost cartoon like. His face was weathered, bearded, and severe. He was brusque and spoke in short, abrupt sentences. When he laughed—infrequently—it made people uneasy.

Everyone knew Cody. They knew that in his younger years he had been a boatman on the Cour d'Alene River in Idaho. He still had the stocky build of a man who had known hard labour and the oars of a scow. But it was the fortune he had made in the gold fields that had brought his fame. The rich vein of pay dirt that ran through his Klondike claim was legendary. There were darker contributions to his fame, too, and his small gang of henchmen was feared.

"Mornin', Cody," a man called from a table near the door. Cody nodded. Another man in a dirty mackinaw called sarcastically from behind the barrel stove, "Any luck last night, Cody?"

Cody smiled mysteriously. "I ain't saying."

The second man persisted. "What's your trick, Cody?" Cody turned away from the man and from the side of his mouth drawled, "Tricks are for whores." Everybody laughed. Cody grinned as he pulled out a battered chair and sat at his usual table, facing the door.

"MaeBeth, I'll have a coffee and eggs," said Cody, before the waitress reached his table. MaeBeth turned on her heel and slipped into the kitchen, only to emerge momentarily with a steaming cup of coffee. Cody pulled a ragged newspaper from his breast pocket. The newspaper was a couple of weeks old and he had read it more times than he cared to. Like everyone else in Dawson City, Cody was eager for break-up, when the paddlewheelers would supply the town. The dog teams did an admirable job, but Skagway was hundreds of miles away and certain things were hard to come by.

Liana rose quietly, walked toward Cody, and sat at his table. "Morning, Cody," said Liana defiantly. Cody feigned fascination with his paper. MaeBeth approached hesitantly, and Liana said, "I'll have what he's having." She moved her chair so that she faced Cody. "Two coffees and scrambled eggs," said MaeBeth.

Cody slowly leaned back in his chair, lowered his paper, folded it, and looked Liana in the eye. "And to what do I owe the pleasure of your company?" he said.

Liana whispered fiercely, "You know why I'm here."

"I forgot my manners," Cody scowled. "Henry was a fine man."

"You heartless son of bitch. Why would you do such a thing?" Liana said, keeping her voice controlled to a whisper so others would not overhear their conversation.

"You're not suggesting I had anything to do with that tragedy?" Cody said menacingly.

"Those were your men. I've seen them hanging around your saloon."

"I ain't saying nothing…but yeah, I knew those men," said Cody, filling his mouth with coffee.

"Why did they come after us?" Liana asked.

"Henry knew what he was doing when he took you. He had no business interfering. He knew what time it was. He's a Siwash for God's sake. He had no business trying to keep you. He should have kept to his own."

"You didn't have to kill anybody. We could have worked things out."

"Look, I don't know what happened up there but I'm down two men."

"You shouldn't have sent them," said Liana defiantly. "That was just wrong."

Cody suddenly grew angry at Liana's questions. "Listen here, girly," he whispered. "If you don't think I will drag you out of here and show you what's what, you're wrong."

Liana felt her temper rising but took a deep breath and looked around the room at the other men eating their breakfasts. She let the pause lengthen. Then, "What do you want, Cody?"

Cody stared into Liana's eyes intensely. "Look, I'm leaving town and I need to settle up. I grubstaked your Pa and now that he's gone, his claim is mine."

"What do you mean 'it's yours'? My father's name is on the deed, and I'm next of kin," said Liana doggedly.

"Considering the hassle and expense of getting you to do what's right, I think I will help myself to the whole thing," Cody said, leaning back in his chair.

"And what about me?" asked Liana, realizing that she was looking into the face of the man who had ordered the death of her father.

"Don't worry about that," said Cody, crossing his arms. "You can leave in one pretty piece. But I will need you to sign that deed over to me. There's a syndicate that wants to buy it. We assumed that you was dead. All the paperwork is ready to go at the Mining Recorder's Office."

Hatred ran through Liana's veins as she remembered her father saying that Cody wanted him to sell his claim to a mining company. It was one of the last conversations they had. Liana pleaded with her father to take the money so they could move away from the Yukon, but her father said the claim would be worth more once it was proven. His body was found a day later, tangled in a logjam on a creek near his claim. Without evidence to the contrary, the authorities ruled he was the apparent victim of a botched creek crossing. Henry knew it wasn't an accident, though, and got Liana away from Dawson City as quick as he could.

"Henry and my father were good folk. You shouldn't have sent your men. It wasn't—"

Cody interrupted. "I'm not saying nothing," he said menacingly. "But nobody crosses me. Nobody. Anyway, I think we've already had this conversation." He crumpled his napkin and crossed his arms. "One way or another, I will get my money. Dawson City is through and I'm moving on."

"And we're just a piece of that?" stammered Liana.

"You owe me because your daddy owed me. You can't quit. Nobody gets to quit. Do yourself a favour," he drawled with mock boredom, "and sign over the deed tomorrow when the offices are open. I suggest you clean yourself up. You even look like a Siwash."

"You'll pay for what you've done," she vowed, shooting a glare.

Cody snickered. "You're just a girl with no men around to protect you; don't make promises you can't keep."

"You heartless son of a bitch!" blurted Liana in disgust.

Continuing in a low tone, Cody seethed, "Listen, girly, I'm feeling generous. You get to walk away." And then in a loud voice to the entire room, he exclaimed, "I'm feeling very generous today. MaeBeth, everybody's breakfast is on me." The room erupted with a cheer for his good graces. "As for you, Lady, I suggest you be smarter than your father or that Siwash friend of his," said Cody with mock sincerity.

"Cody, you've made a terrible mistake," Liana promised with a stony grimace.

"The only mistake I made was assuming you was dead."

Liana looked at the brightening streets through the streaked glass windows. Three ravens were tormenting a dog tied to a post. They bounced on the snow mere inches from the extent of the mutt's line. The dog brayed and lunged but was unable to reach them. MaeBeth slid two plates of eggs and toast across the table. As he picked up his fork, Cody smiled at Liana.

"I suggest you hire your passage. I'm not looking over my shoulder because of no crazy bitch." He grinned. "I'll give you a couple of days to get out of town. Now, I'm hungry. Let's eat up while it's hot."

Silently he shovelled the reconstituted powdered eggs into his mouth and dipped his sourdough toast into his coffee. Within a minute his plate was clean. He dropped a nugget the size of his thumb on the table and rose to his feet. He stretched his arms and then tipped his hat to Liana.

"Remember, two days. That's all. And don't forget to transfer the deed to me. You don't want to want to have an accident like your Pa." This statement reconfirmed what Liana already knew but her heart still sank to hear him say it. A scowl creased her forehead.

"Don't be a fool," added Cody, standing and putting on his parka. "Know when you're beat." He turned and stomped to the door. The other patrons all tried to meet his eyes with a nod. Liana intently watched his flamboyance, his confidence.

Liana sat in her chair, considering her options. After a while she absentmindedly ate her eggs and toast. Her head swam with Cody's threats and his admission of everything she had assumed. She knew what she had to do. When she was finished eating, she stood and paid with a single gold nugget. She pulled on her coat and made her way through the tables to the door. Nobody paid her any notice. Liana wondered why they didn't notice the wolf's cry. It seemed so close and loud. It almost seemed as though the wolf was in the hotel, but she couldn't see it anywhere.

Liana crossed the icy dirt street to Bacson's Dry Goods. The shopkeeper had just opened and was pleased to see Liana. "You're my first customer of the day," he said by way of greeting.

Liana smiled. "I'm looking for a small leg-hold trap and some black shoe polish."

"Sure, we have plenty," said the shopkeeper, walking past a barrel of salt pork and reaching to a cluster of traps hanging off a single nail on the wall. "Here you go," he said, handing the trap to Liana and turning to rummage for a tin of shoe polish.

"Will you be needing anything else?" he inquired, placing the shoe polish on the counter.

"Some snare wire," said Liana. She pointed at a small coil on a nail next to the traps on the wall. She hesitated, then picked through a pile of work clothes for a few minutes. "I will take these pants and these shirts and this coat," said Liana, lifting the clothing onto the counter.

"Is that all you'll be needing?"

"I will also need some food delivered to a cabin up the river," Liana said. "I don't know whose cabin it is, but I ate everything he had," smiled Liana. "I know you can handle it."

Used to this kind of directive, the shopkeeper placed a map on the counter and asked Liana to mark the cabin's location. Liana quickly found the canyon that was marked with little squiggly wave symbols and straight parallel lines. The island wasn't marked on the map, but Liana was able to fairly accurately deduce the distance of the cabin from the bottom of the canyon. "Tell whoever goes up there that if they reach the canyon, they've gone too far."

The man smiled with amusement while he lifted a canvas bag to pack the purchases. "I need to replace a lot of tinned goods," she continued. "Stew and cherries mainly. And throw in a box of matches." Liana collected a large assortment of goods she had either eaten or craved when she was at the cabin. She passed the map back to the shopkeeper and he promised to have the provisions delivered by dog team within a couple of weeks. Liana felt good replacing the food but shuddered at the thought of eating canned stew or canned cherries ever again.

"Will that be all?" asked the shopkeeper again.

"Yes, that's it," said Liana, taking the trap and inspecting it in the weak winter sunlight coming in the front window.

"Will you be needing any bait? I've got some dried salmon the martens can't keep away from."

"I don't think so. Just this stuff, and please make sure to deliver the canned goods to that cabin," she said, handing a few nuggets to the man. The man smiled broadly as he pulled a scale from behind the counter to weigh the nuggets and make change. "That won't be necessary," said Liana, opening the door.

"Have a good day," said the shopkeeper cheerfully, calculating his substantial tip.

Liana stepped into the crisp morning air and stowed the trap and shoe polish deep in her big jacket pocket. She looked in both directions and decided to walk down Broadway. The snow was piled loose in the road and many of the boardwalks were clear. Narrow paths twisted through waist deep banks of snow to stores, cabins, and tents. Her breath held heavy in the brisk morning air and she walked deliberately. The town was still waking, and few people were about.

At the end of Fourth Street, Liana spotted Cody's house on a steep hillside. It was a log cabin, slightly bigger than most. The cabin had two small windows in the front, trimmed with white lace curtains. A dark green door boasted a brass knocker shaped like an upside-down fist. It was a modest home for someone as rich and powerful as Cody, but he had another house in Seattle said to be one of the grandest painted ladies on the west coast. His wife and kids lived there, but he hadn't seen them in years.

Liana stood under a large spruce tree a half block away. She stashed her bag of new clothes between the roots and opened the tin of shoe polish. She started to spread it on the metal trap. The cold made spreading the paste difficult, but Liana was able to coat the trap with thick, dark clumps. In a few minutes the trap was entirely covered in the thick grease.

Liana walked toward Cody's place. She slipped silently through the open gate and into the back yard along a narrow path that lead to the outhouse. She smiled, remembering Henry's comments about the outhouse at the cabin being ten yards too far from the cabin in the winter and ten yards too close in the summer.

After the trap was set, Liana left Cody's yard. She looked back at the cabin and felt conflicted. Henry had never told any stories about revenge. As she stood under the spruce tree, she felt a momentary pang of regret. But Cody had taken so much from her she didn't feel enough remorse to alter her decision. Not wanting to draw attention to herself, she turned to walk back downtown.

The sun was higher in the sky and Liana's stomach was declaring itself hungry again. She walked the boardwalk until she saw a tent restaurant selling donuts and coffee. She pushed back the canvas flap and sat at a long bench with several men. The tent was warm and unbearably humid. A woodstove crackled and popped. The men all had straggly beards and the sallow faces of veteran Stampeders—hungry and exhausted.

She asked the cook for a basin and some soap. He warned her she would incur a nickel surcharge. Liana nodded. Within moments, an enameled metal basin of warm water slid across the table toward her. Liana submerged her blackened hands into the lukewarm water with an inaudible gasp. The harsh lye soap and shoe polish quickly turned the water an opaque, oily mess. When her hands were cleaner, she stood and carried the basin outside, where she threw the water into the snow and wiped her hands dry on her pants. Returning to the tent, she thanked the cook and sat at the table to sip coffee and quietly enjoy a donut.

The men were discussing a new survey. The chief surveyor was already hiring a line crew to help make sense of the imprecise staking of the gold claims during the previous winter. The men were optimistic that there would be some valuable "fractions" as a result. As this was important talk of gold, nobody really noticed Liana and she didn't say anything until she paid. Once again she took a small nugget from her pocket and smiled as she emerged into the brightness of the cold morning.

Liana trudged toward a yard behind the police barracks near the river. Before she got within spitting distance of the yard, huskies began to howl and bark at her approach. Fifty or sixty dogs were chained to trees and beside them sat a lone white canvas tent with a black stovepipe thrusting above it. In front of each dog was a metal bucket or bowl. Two or three of the dogs slept curled in the snow, their tails over their noses to keep them warm. But the rest of the dogs barked and howled and jumped at the end of their chains. Liana stood at the front of the tent, where dog sleds rested against log supports.

"Hello. I'm looking for Nelson," she called above the din.

"He's gone. He's outside for the winter. Got sick," said a youthful voice from within the tent.

"Well, can I talk to you about hiring a team then?" asked Liana.

"Sure, we can talk. C'mon in," instructed the voice.

Liana pulled away the heavy tent flap and stepped into the warm, dark interior. Sitting in the corner on a pile of furs was a boy, perhaps sixteen or seventeen.

"I'm Nelson's nephew, Drake," he said.

"Hi. I'm Liana."

"You look familiar."

"I once lived in Dawson," she answered haltingly. "It was a long time ago."

"Where're you headed?" Drake asked.

"The coast, and I have to leave today."

"Why now? There's a horse sleigh going out on Friday. You should take the Royal Mail. It'd be safer."

"No. I have to leave now," she insisted. "I can't say why and nobody can know that you are taking me—for both our sakes."

"Sounds intriguing," he drawled.

"Can you do it? Can you take me out?" asked Liana insistently.

"Of course I can, but it will cost you," Drake said.

"I don't care about the cost. I care about leaving as soon as we can."

"Well, I can get you to Anderson Roadhouse tonight. I usually skip about half the road houses, and if the weather isn't too cold, we can even run in shifts with lanterns."

Liana felt a sense of relief wash over her frame. "That sounds good. How many dogs will we bring?"

"How much stuff are you carrying?" he asked.

"Just what I'm wearing. I travel light."

"It will cost you a hundred plus meals and lodging at the roadhouses," he said confidently. "I need to take some dried salmon for the dogs; that'll cost. But we'll be in Whitehorse in no time."

"That sounds good," said Liana. "Can I help you get things prepared?"

"Yeah, you can water the dogs. Start by going to the river. There's an auger beside the little red flag on the river." He looked at Liana and doubted her experience with an auger. "It was opened last night so you probably will only have a couple of inches of ice to cut."

"I'm sorry, but I can't risk being seen with you. Is there anything inside I can do?"

"You really are on the run," said Drake, somewhat surprised.

"Let's just leave it at that. Tell me how much salmon you need; I'll arrange for that and pay for it. Then I'll walk outside of town toward the creeks. I will meet you where the Klondike meets the Yukon."

"That path is well travelled. You may want to wait until after dark," suggested Drake.

"How about if we meet at seven at the forks?" she said.

"That will work. For now, why don't you go back to my cabin and make up some beaver and rice for the dogs," said Drake, pointing to his cabin next door. "We'll freeze what they don't eat and take it with us."

"I can do that," replied Liana, pleased to have something useful to do.

"The beaver meat is in the cache."

Liana handled the salmon order, then went to the cabin and lifted an enormous bucket on top of the stove after filling it with snow. Eagerly she climbed a narrow ladder to a cache about a dozen feet off the ground. She pushed open a small hatch and reached around in the dark until she found the beaver meat. Once inside the cabin, she dumped the meat into the pot; it was dark and rich with fat. Liana thought about how welcome this meat would have been on the island. She left the improvised pot to cook and walked back to town.

Liana thought about going back to the hotel and looking for any acquaintances but reasoned that some might be working for Cody. She knew at least one of them sometimes slept in his bed. "If it wasn't for Henry," she thought, "I would be in the cemetery above town—or rotting out in the underbrush."

She knew it was best to get out of town before Cody even knew she was gone. But first she went to a washhouse and asked for a bath. She gave the attendant a nugget and took a towel and a bar of soap. She walked into a tiny room that held a huge tin tub full of steaming water. The window was covered in a thick layer of ice that kept her privacy from the outside and filtered a thin, translucent glow in the bright afternoon sunlight. She quickly stripped and dangled a foot in the scalding water. When she lowered herself into the tub, she felt overwhelmed and lost her breath. She spent the next hour turning the water a grayish hue. Once the bath had cooled to lukewarm, she dried herself and dressed in the new clothes. She tossed her grimy old duds in the corner to be thrown out and inspected herself in a mirror hanging on the wall. She turned to view the scars on each of her hips and smiled broadly. Liana could hear a wolf calling somewhere from the street below.

Liana walked out of the washhouse a new person. Her neatly coiled hair steamed in the cold and she proudly strode down the street. She returned to Drake's tent and asked if she could help prepare the dogs. He commented that she looked different; Liana surprised herself with a blush. Drake had her ladle scoops of warm broth and beaver meat into the dogs' bowls. They in turn howled in frenzy, their lips quivering in anticipation. The smell of the stew made Liana choke but to the dogs it was nirvana. They liked salmon head stew even better, Drake told her. Drake carried the nourishing meal to the screaming huskies while Liana watched from the cabin. One dog looked like a wolf and Liana walked closer to see. It was larger than the other dogs.

"Drake, is that one a wolf?" she asked.

"Blue, well, half of her is," he said proudly. "When her Ma was in heat, a wolf pack was in the area." They watched Blue devour her food. "We're lucky they didn't just leave a collar. That's happened a lot around here."

"She looks one hundred percent wolf," said Liana.

"Everybody thinks so," Drake continued. "Makes some people uncomfortable. I once caught a guy in the yard that wanted her hide," he said, shaking his head. "Worth a lot of money, she is."

Liana couldn't stop staring at Blue. "She's beautiful."

"If it was up to me we would have kept the litter," he said wistfully, "but all we kept was Blue. The best lead dog in the Yukon, I figure."

Drake walked away from the dogs and began to prepare the sled and the lines. He inspected the runners and joints and positioned a couple of dusty caribou hides in the basket for Liana to sit on, as well as a buffalo robe to cover her. He laid out the dogs' harnesses and attachments in front of the sled. Testing, Drake stepped on the sled's brake and threw an anchor into the snow. That accomplished, he suggested they go up the street for pork and beans and waffles.

"You'll feel better starting out with a good feed in your belly," Drake explained. "Nobody will think anything about it. They all think I'm too young to run a sled."

"I guess it's a good idea," replied Liana, her stomach grumbling. "But we can't risk being seen together. Instead, why don't you go and get us something and we can eat it here," she suggested, handing Drake a nugget. He left the cabin and returned several minutes later with a steaming butter bucket full of beans and a stack of waffles wrapped in a faded cloth.

They sat at the table in the cabin and Drake served two enormous bowls of beans and pork that smelled only slightly less offensive than the slop the dogs had gulped down. A greasy film coated the top of the bowl. Drake ate his in large mouthfuls that he washed down with cups of weak black coffee diluted with evaporated milk. Liana watched in amazement as this wraith of a boy ate bowl after bowl; she could swallow only a single serving before feeling stuffed. As he finished his last helping, Drake used a waffle to wipe his mouth and the dregs, and then hungrily devoured it as well. Leftover waffles went into his pocket.

Drake then began the final preparations as Liana walked out under the darkening sky. The dogs began to howl in anticipation as soon as they saw Drake walking toward the river. The sound was deafening, yet did not draw any attention from the townsfolk, who were used to the cacophony of canines. Liana thought about the wolves and the way they sang in unison.

Walking away from town felt good to Liana. Within ten minutes she was in the darkened forest and away from prying eyes. As she walked she thought about Cody and his small world. The heyday of Dawson City was over, and Liana thought this was a good thing. She followed a trail rutted with footprints and wagon wheels. She covered the few miles with miraculously little effort, and as she approached the forks of the river she could see Drake's lantern on the Yukon. The dogs were silent.

Drake took off his rucksack and placed it in the sled. "You can sit on that later if you want." Liana could see the nine dogs attached to the sled in the lamplight. Blue's head seemed thinner and more angular than it had in town, and even in the lantern light Liana could see she had bright blue eyes. Having Blue in front comforted Liana and she settled into Drake's confidence that everything was going to be all right.

"I'll walk in front of them until we get going," Drake said. "Why don't you unhook the anchor and walk behind until we're sorted?"

Liana pulled up the snow anchor and hooked it into the litter. Drake started running the team on a trail along the river. "Jump in!" he yelled. Liana flopped into the front of the sled on the buffalo hides. The team quickly began to pass Drake, who climbed onto the back of the sled as it pulled up adjacent to him and balanced his feet on its skis.

"Gee! Gee!" Drake hollered, and Blue led the team to the right, away from the forest.

Liana looked behind her toward Dawson City. She could make out the faint glow of lights on the mountain ridges behind town. "Good riddance!" yelled Liana. The dog sled glided toward the coast. Liana huddled in her parka and thought about Henry and everything she had gone through. *Thanks for sharing your stories, Henry; I haven't disappointed you.*

★★★

Cody woke early the next day and sat up in the darkness of the arctic morning. Sleeping next to him was one of his "entertainers." She barely stirred under the heavy quilts as Cody slipped out of bed. He pulled a fur coat over his red, full body long johns and stepped into a pair of knee-high boots he kept next to the door. In the North, women used chamber pots, but men like Cody always used outhouses.

Cody stumbled into the cold twilight and briskly walked along the backyard path to the outhouse. He opened the door, turned, hung his coat on a ten-penny nail, and dropped the buttoned panel covering his behind. He winced at the cold as he sat on the frigid wooden seat. He tried to produce as quickly as possible and within moments was successful. His steaming feces dropped into the abyss but connected with resistance. Instantaneously, a loud snap rang in the morning's silence. Before he could summon a thought, Cody felt his testicles sever in the metal trap's teeth. He fell forward into the daylight, drooling a guttural moan, paralyzed by shock and pain. He rocked in the snow momentarily and then mercifully blacked out. The snow at the outhouse door steamed with bright blood. The pale sky above the distant mountains was dull under a bright sliver of sun.

Liana squinted in the brightness, the wolf's cry filling her soul. She realized that she was back on the island. In that instant she had lived a lifetime and glimpsed what was possible. She was hurtling over the steely river with her right leg pointed toward the ice on the far side. She shrieked a mad groan as she arced over the gap and away from the miserable little island. She knew she was close to escaping the solitude and the bottomless cold.

As the toes of her right foot glanced the snow on the bank, Liana felt her other leg start to drag into the river. Instinctively she bent her torso toward the forest and tried to grab the ice. Her foot and then leg broke the surface of the river as she madly tried to grasp its hard surface. Her efforts were fruitless; Liana spun backwards and with an angry splash was swallowed by the river.

Liana slumped into the dense cold of the river. The icy water enveloped her with barely a whisper. Her limp body slowly dropped to the bottom and she bounced off the gravel in disbelief. Mercilessly, her body bobbed to the surface, where her face emerged from the river for a single defeated breath. The undulating tide turned her face to the faded sky. She did not try to swim to either shore.

Liana could see the wolf standing at the edge of the forest. His sorrowful eyes met hers with the compassion of a friend. The wolf raised its head to the pale sky and cried a last howl for Liana. She felt grateful for the wolf waking her from her icy slumber and giving her hope and a chance of escape. The wolf soon dropped its head to watch Liana disappear downstream.

Liana drifted down the lead between the icy banks for a few moments. The valley was quiet except for her heavy breaths and the pounding of her heart. Liana thought about her mother and father and Henry and remembered a kinder time.

"I can't wait to hear your voices again!" she hollered to the sky. Her voice echoed downriver and trailed off into the forest. She closed her eyes and thought about how close she had come to surviving the island. She heard the raven and the wolves and the snowstorm and felt the dull fire in the sky shine on her plaintive lips. Her sallow frame spun in the slow current of the river, and when she opened her eyes she felt the hunger of her heart.

www.ingramcontent.com/pod-product-compliance
Lightning Source LLC
Chambersburg PA
CBHW070555180626
46817CB00005B/1854